CHRISTOPHER PIKE

THE STARLIGHT CRYSTAL

Hodder
Children's
Books

a division of Hodder Headline plc

Copyright © 1996 Christopher Pike

First published in the USA in 1996
by Pocket Books, a division of Simon & Schuster Inc.

First published in Great Britain in 1996
by Hodder Children's Books

The right of Christopher Pike to be identified as the Author
of the Work has been asserted by him in accordance with
the Copyright, Designs and Patents Act 1988.

10 9 8 7 6 5 4 3 2 1

A Catalogue record for this book is available
from the British Library

ISBN 0 340 61914 7

Typeset by Avon Dataset Ltd, Bidford-on-Avon, Warks

Printed and bound in Great Britain by
Cox & Wyman, Reading, Berks

Hodder Children's Books
a division of Hodder Headline plc
338 Euston Road
London NW1 3BH

For Paige Christian

1

How do I explain a life that has lasted for billions of years? It is almost as if I must start with an apology for being alive when everyone I once knew is dead. But because my love for them still lives, I believe their souls forgive me. But does the universe? I wonder. I have watched even the stars change, as their energies dwindle and their light dims. I love them as well. They are all I have left—the stars and the memory of the many times I wished upon them. But with all those wishes, I asked for only one thing.

To see him again.

But I will not see him. I do not see him now.

There is only the dust of a ruined world. The salt of dead seas. I taste the salt on my parched lips, and I feel so terribly alone. Yes, despite my love, I believe the stars have cursed me for trying to outlast them. Nine billion years and the only lesson

I've learned is a bitter one. I should have known at the beginning, when I said goodbye to him.

I should have known not to go.

But I knew nothing. That day we met.

Except that I was happy.

It was a Sunday. I was at the library reading history—the late twentieth century. That was an interesting time for an eighteen-year-old like myself. But unlike a student in those crazy days two hundred years ago, I was not studying by reading a book or watching a video. I was hooked up to a Hypno-Prompt, a century-old invention that was capable of feeding an encyclopedia of information into my mind in the space of two hours.

The machine first put me into a deep hypnotic state, so my mind could absorb facts like a sponge soaking up water. The machine consisted of headgear that went across my face. A learning session usually started with a blank screen and the faint roar of waves or the gentle pelting of rain. Slowly the natural sounds lulled me into a peaceful state.

The screen was not a screen in the traditional sense. Two blunt-ended fiber optics led to each of my eyes. These optics fired images directly into my brain at a speed my conscious mind couldn't follow, but which my subconscious could. I enjoyed sessions with the Hypno-Prompt. They were always relaxing and, of course, incredibly informative. But they scared me as well. I took in such huge blocks of knowledge in such short periods that I wasn't sure I was the same person afterward. Leaving the library that day, a kaleidoscope of "nineteen nineties" images spun in my brain.

There were riots in the streets back then. People became celebrities for committing murder. Politicians were trying to legislate morality. Popular music was urging people to kill authority figures. It was an insane era.

Yet it was filled with great beauty and excitement. There were major medical breakthroughs every other day. The first steps into outer space were being taken. Art and music were often crude, but almost always inventive. The majority of politicians may have been misled, but many were trying to create a better society. To me, the late twentieth century was the worst of times and the best of times. As I left the library to meet my destiny, I decided I would have been very happy to be alive then.

"Been a long time since I rock and rolled," I sang as I hurried down the library steps. Where had the lyrics come from? It was some kind of heavy metal song from a group called Heavy Balloon. Something like that. It usually took me a few hours to assimilate everything the Hypno-Prompt had crammed into my skull.

There was a young woman standing on the steps, as I came out.

She was staring at me. As if she knew me, knew me well.

But I'd never seen her before.

She stepped toward me. Her sunglasses were wide and dark, her blond hair short and stiff as if it had been dyed with harsh chemicals. She had my thin build and was about my height, but her features were hard. Her age was difficult to guess— she could have been a year older or ten. She walked as if she had been through a lot in her life; stiffly, a bit wearily. Yet she smiled as she neared me, and offered me her hand.

"You look like you don't remember me, Paige," she said in a soft voice. "I met you a couple years ago. We were introduced at a party for a mutual friend. My name's Alpha Book."

I shook her hand. "I'm sorry. I know your face, but that's all." I didn't really know her face. But there was something about her that made me feel we had met before. "Who was the friend?"

She smiled quickly. It seemed forced. Her eyes strayed to Rainbow Park, which was across the street. "I don't remember. Isn't that funny? But I do remember you." She pointed to the park. "I was just there. It's lovely today. You should go. I was sitting by the lake beside the fountain." She lowered her head and sorrow touched her features, although it was difficult to see how deep it went because of her dark glasses. She added, "It was very lovely."

I didn't know what to make of her. "I've never heard the name Alpha before."

She looked up. "It suits me, Paige." Then she

reached in her coat, and for a moment I sensed danger and was afraid. In fact, I had the ridiculous idea that she was about to pull out a gun and shoot me. I stiffened, ready to flee. But all she withdrew was a handkerchief. She touched it to her eyes without removing her glasses. "I should go," she said, nodding to me. "It was nice to see you again."

"You, too," I said.

I watched her as she headed down the steps and then disappeared around the side of the building. She had only come to tell me to go to the park, I realized. How odd.

I went because I was curious. To the spot she described.

It was not a sacrifice. I might have gone anyway. Rainbow Park was my favorite place on the entire west coast of America. It was unlike any park a teenager from the late twentieth century would have known. For one thing it was larger than parks had been—ten miles across—and covered with trees from all over the world, man-made mountains, and splashing waterfalls. Never mind the five thousand varieties of birds and the five different species of bears who lived there. Rainbow Park stood right in the center of what had once been Los Angeles, which had been leveled by a massive earthquake in the early twenty-first century.

At the lake, close to the fountain, I saw no one.

At least not at first. But then Tem appeared.

He came right up out of the water. He wore scuba equipment—he had just been diving. His sudden appearance startled me. I got up from where I was sitting and started to move away as he walked out of the water in my direction. But then he removed his face mask and smiled.

"You don't look like a fish," he said.

"In case you didn't notice, you've already surfaced," I said.

He took a step closer, dripping on the grass. His hair was long and dark; he wore it in braids down to his waist, the popular custom. His face was also dark: he looked half Indian, a quarter African, maybe a little Irish. His eyes were a startling blue, even under a film of evaporating water. He was tall, well muscled, and moved with carefree grace. He couldn't have been more than two years older than I was. I had to shield my eyes as I stared up at him because he had the sun at his back. Always, to me, I would remember Tem moving with light. He tossed aside his mask and studied me.

"But you do look like a mermaid," he said. "You know what that is?"

"Of course. And you look like a big toad. Do you know what that is?"

He threw his head back and laughed. "You know, most guys would be insulted by that remark. But I take it as a compliment."

"Why? I am trying to insult you."

He continued to smile. "I love frogs. They're one of my major fields of study." He offered his hand. "I'm Tem."

I shook my head. "I can't shake your hand. You might give me toad warts."

6

"That's impossible. And even if I do, you can just have them frozen off."

"The cost sounds a little high to me." I paused. "Hey, did you see a young woman around here before you went under?"

"No."

"Anyone?"

"No. Why?"

"It doesn't matter." I pointed to the water. "What were you doing in there anyway?"

"Studying frogs."

"Seriously?"

"Yes. They haven't been chirping as loud this year as last. I'm trying to find out why."

"Do you have any theories?"

"Yes." He moved closer and spoke confidentially. "I think it's because there are more boy frogs in the lake than girl frogs. I think both sexes are frustrated."

I laughed. "If you weren't so good-looking I'd think that was a pick-up line."

"You're not bad looking yourself."

"Your compliment means nothing. You love the sight of frogs."

But I glowed at his compliment. One thing that hadn't changed since the end of the twentieth century was the vanity of eighteen-year-old girls. I was usually quite confident about my looks—that is, except when I was standing beside a cute guy. I was tall and thin and could eat all I wanted and never gain a pound. My hair was dark red, the color of desert dusk; I usually wore it layered to my shoulders. My green eyes were my best feature, according to my father, who seldom complimented me. I sometimes wondered if he said that because I had inherited my eyes from him. But I doubted it—vanity was never one of his weaknesses. Captain Karl Christian—people shook when he walked by, his commanding aura was so imposing.

Tem offered his hand again. "Come on. What're a few warts between friends?"

I hesitated, then shook his hand. "You don't even know my name. How can you call yourself my friend?"

"I know you." He leaned over and kissed my hand lightly. "I don't need your name to know I know you."

And I did know him. I don't know how. He was a stranger—handsome, true, but not someone I ordinarily would have been attracted to. He was too weird, for one thing, and I was the last person who needed to start a romance. I was a week away from leaving the earth for two hundred years aboard the *Traveler*. Whoever I met now would be dead when I returned. While I would have aged only one year. Einstein's Theory of Relativity would see to that.

I wanted to tell Tem right then as he kissed my hand. That he was wasting my time because we would soon be on drastically different clocks. Then he straightened up and stared into my eyes, and I swear I felt so much love for him then that it was either a miracle of God or a lapse in sanity. I did not believe in reincarnation. I'm not sure if I do now, at least not in the way established religions describe it. But another life is the only way I can explain how much it meant to meet him. I felt as we gazed at each other as if I were peering into a corridor of blessed souls, a labyrinth of blissful life that had no beginning or end. I felt happy right then, in a way I had never known before.

And I also felt sad, in a way I was to know too well too soon.

"I'm Paige," I whispered.

He was serious, for once. "Are you the first page, or the last?"

I didn't answer, not right then.

But I told him later that I was leaving soon. In one week.

2

And a week later we stood in the exact spot.

He wanted to follow me up into orbit to say goodbye, but I said no. In the last seven days, we had spent every waking moment together, mainly outside in the sun, and I wanted to remember him as I remembered the earth—full of life and warmth. For some reason, I was afraid to connect our time together to the cold and blackness of space. Tem didn't understand but he respected my wish. We respected each other a great deal by then.

He kissed me beside the lake and held me close.

"I love you," he said.

But I turned away and stared at the water. "I wish you didn't," I whispered.

He touched my shoulder. "Why?"

The sun was close to the horizon. Reflected on the water, it made the whole lake a bowl of blood. "You know why," I said. "The next time I stand on this world, I will stand beside your grave."

"You can bring me flowers."

I turned to him. "I can't bear the thought. Don't you see?"

He saw that I was in pain. He hugged me again. "I have been thinking about how fast time will fly for you, and how slow it will pass for me. And I have a plan. We can defeat time." He lifted up my chin, forcing me to stare into his eyes. "Listen to me, Paige, our love can beat it."

I had to smile. He was full of plans. "What is it?"

"I know the acceleration of the *Traveler* will disallow regular radio contact, but we can still communicate. Our relationship can go on. We can take a vow, you and I. I will write you once a month on my computer. You will write me once a month on yours. Of course, you will have all my letters after a short time, but if you promise not to read them until each of your months has passed, it will be like we're having a long distance affair."

I liked the idea. "But you won't get to see all my letters." Because I had to, I added, "You'll be dead."

He pulled me tighter. "I'll see all your letters."

"How?"

"That's for me to know. You just keep your end of the bargain. As your ship reaches near light speed, and the years fly by, and all my letters tumble in at once, please don't read ahead. That's all you have to promise me."

I nodded. "I promise, Tem. But you must promise you won't forget me."

He spoke with feeling. "I will never forget you."

"Never is a long time," I whispered in his ear.

"Not for us."

"If we only had more time."

"Time is nothing to us, Paige. This moment is forever."

"Forever," I mumbled, feeling a peculiar chill. Stepping back, I removed a small knife from my pocket and cut off a lock of my red hair. I gave it to him. "I want you to have this." I gestured to his hair. "I want a lock of yours."

He let me take it. Then he kissed me again. His touch was *so* good.

I shed only one tear, but it was as heavy as gold.

Finally I had to pull away. My watch demanded it.

"Goodbye, Tem."

He smiled at me. "Goodbye, Paige."

I turned and walked away. I glanced over my shoulder only once, but he stood with his back to me, his feet in the water, his eyes on the setting sun. The red light did indeed resemble blood, the end of all things. It was to burn in my soul like a memory etched in the twilight of a youth who had never known innocence. The sun set even as I watched him, and he was lost in shadows.

"Goodbye, my love," I said softly.

3

The *Traveler* resembled a huge spear, aimed at the next two centuries. Over a half mile long and a hundred yards wide, it was equipped to carry over six hundred crew members. The entire rear half of the vessel was devoted to the recently developed graviton drive, which could bend and focus the waves of gravity that crisscrossed the universe and use them as a means of propulsion. It was like riding the crests of all the oceans' waves. The *Traveler* would take six months to accelerate to near light speed, where time itself would begin to do an exotic dance. It was a time capsule as well as a spaceship, and it would be my home for the next year and ten days of my life. All because my father, Commander Karl Christian, was the ship's captain.

The purpose of our mission was simple—to observe human society over a perspective of two centuries, and then return home. Our orbit would take us above the plane of the cometary cloud, which lay beyond Pluto. Around and around we would circle the solar system, our many instruments pointed toward the warmth of the sun, traveling through the years, but never really going anywhere in space.

Of course we would see nothing earth didn't see. Earth would record the same history as we would. But what we would bring back to earth was a *perspective* of the two centuries past, a bit of living history. *We* would be the history. We were mankind's insurance that it would lose nothing that it had gained until then.

Sometimes, though, I thought our published purpose was abstract. Sometimes I thought we were going out there because mankind was nervous. Nervous about what it would run into now that it had just begun to explore the stars. We were insurance, yes, maybe life insurance.

Yet while we were in the acceleration phase, as Tem had noted, our instruments wouldn't work very well. The graviton drive distorted space itself. We could only receive messages from earth when the drive was turned off. Otherwise, we would fly in oblivion, unaware of what was happening to humanity. But six months of accelerating, and another six months decelerating, was not considered too long a time to be out of reach. Not when our mission was so lengthy.

When measured by an outside stationary observer's standards.

That was the key.

It all went back to Einstein. That guy had been one smart cookie. He had figured out the most famous equation of them all: $E = mc^2$—energy equals mass times the velocity of light squared. What that meant for us was that as we neared the speed of light—to an outside observer—our mass and therefore our kinetic energy would near infinity. Yet aboard the *Traveler* we wouldn't feel especially heavy or infinite. Nor would we notice that time had slowed down for us. Yet in that last one percent of velocity—between ninety-nine percent the speed of light and one hundred percent—time could slow down until it practically came to a stop.

Unfortunately, for me, for my heart, the six months of acceleration were crucial. Once we reached our desired velocity and remained there for ten days, two hundred years on earth would fly by. Tem would age years in my minutes. He would write me dozens of letters—one every month—while I brushed my teeth one morning. For me and my fellow travelers, the two hundred years would pass in ten days, and in those ten days all our instruments would be humming with activity.

It was in those ten days Tem would die.

I wondered if I would know it. The actual instant he died.

My father met me as I came aboard. He kissed me on the right cheek rather mechanically. My father was not known for displays of affection. Yet distant relatives said that when my mother was alive, he had been much warmer. But those days I didn't remember. My mother had perished from an unexpected solar flare, while doing sun research inside the orbit of Mercury. From pictures, I knew we looked very much alike. I wondered if that was one of the reasons my father and I were never close. If I was a ghost that never quit haunting him.

Yet I loved my father. His inner strength showed in his outer build. He was stocky but not short. His features were squarish, seemingly cut by rulers and computers rather than by nature. His green eyes were the same as mine in color and shape, but the power that radiated behind them was a wonder itself. He didn't have to open his mouth to give an order. His glance said more than most peoples' words. In defiance of recent tastes, he kept his head completely shaved. It suited him; it brought him that much closer to being a machine.

I didn't know if my father loved me.

"How was your flight up?" he asked, looking smart in his black uniform. I wore a purple uniform, as did most relations of officers. Purple was at the bottom of the authority ladder, not that I cared. About half the crew members had family with them. The government understood how hard two centuries apart could be on a family.

I had asked that Tem be allowed to come with me. I had begged.

But my father said there was no room for him.

Did I hate him for that? I don't know.

Tem had begged me to stay and I had refused.

What right did I have to hate anyone?

I forced a smile. "My flight up was lovely. How is the ship? Are we ready to take off?"

"Yes." My father turned and walked toward the bridge. I followed. "You're the last one to board. We leave within the hour." He paused. "Did you enjoy your last week?"

He was asking many things with the question. He knew I had met Tem, had wanted to bring him along. Yet he had no idea how deep my love ran. I saw no reason to burden him with my pain. As captain, he already had too much to oversee. I forced another smile, kept my voice light.

"I had a lovely time," I said.

"That's nice," he answered.

4

We left earth orbit. Even plowing out from the sun, we accelerated rapidly. Yet the graviton drive worked internally as well as externally, balancing the pressure on us fragile biological units. None of us felt the power of our growing speed. Not unless we looked out the window. For me, the sun seemed to fade quickly in brightness, until it was nothing but a bright star shining in an endless sea of stars. Beyond the orbit of Pluto, it was dark and cold.

A month went by and I received Tem's first letter. It was grabbed in the brief hour the graviton drive was turned off for maintenance reasons. That meant my own letter was also sent in that same hour. My note was therefore not a reply to his. We would be a month off with our letters, until such things became meaningless. I read his letter alone in my cabin. It was not long but I treasured every word.

Paige,

I have been very good since you left. I spend all my time with the frogs, trying to repair their sex lives while wondering what to do with my own now that you are gone. Honestly, I haven't been tempted by any of the creatures around me, human or otherwise.

I miss you. What a feeble way to put it, huh? When I think of you, I feel like dying and smiling at the same time. I hope I die with a smile on my face. Maybe I will have myself frozen at that moment, and you can see whether I did or not.

But seriously, I miss you terribly. I study, I eat, I sleep, I go for walks, and most of all I stare up at the sky. Sometimes at night I imagine I see your ship. I see a star twinkle and I think of the glimmer in your eyes when we were alone at night. Really, I think of nothing but you. For me, it will always be this way.

> *Love, and more love,*
> *Tem*

My letter was even shorter.

Tem,

Don't hate me but all I can say right now is that I love you. If I say more, it will have no meaning. Damn, it hurts like hell, but I treasure the pain.

> *Paige*

It was a sort of depressing letter. But misery loves company—I thought he would like it. The thing had taken me a month to write. Amazing how time crumbles when your heart is shattered.

I had two official roles aboard the *Traveler:* first, I was a student of sociology, and second, I worked in the ship's garden. My study of sociology would be of particular help as we reached the midpoint of our trip, when the entire earth society went through a two-century adjustment. I was supposed to learn something at that time, all of mankind was supposed to. I wondered what it would be.

I also enjoyed working in the garden. I especially liked the roses. I was the only one who insisted we grow bushes with thorns. In my depressed state, the only way I could enjoy the flowers was to see the sharp thorns as well as the delicate petals. I saw my work with the roses as a metaphor for my love affair.

5

Kabrina worked in the garden with me.

She was my friend. She was short and soft spoken. Her hair was a golden halo, fine as silk. I loved to brush it, when she'd let me. Her father was my father's First Officer—Number One—the second most powerful man aboard the *Traveler*. Unlike me, Kabrina had both her parents to keep her company, and no boyfriend left behind to grieve over. Yet Kabrina had burdens of her own. Since birth, she had been completely deaf. I spoke to her partially by signing, but mostly by allowing her to read my lips. Kabrina could read lips like no deaf person in the solar system. Sometimes I thought she just read my mind.

Surprisingly she had a lovely voice. Her sentences were halting, but clear. I never had trouble understanding her, and I would say no one understood me as well as Kabrina did. I often talked to her about Tem, and she listened without interruption. There is a special kind of understanding that emerges from silence. Many times we would work for hours in the garden, and I would feel no need to speak. It was enough to know she was there beside me.

That day, after receiving Tem's first letter, I plucked a red rose and a thorn stabbed me in my thumb. The blood spilled into my palm. I just stood and stared at it. This was one metaphor I didn't care for. Kabrina came up beside me and took my hand.

"Do you want some disinfectant?" she asked quietly. Kabrina never spoke above a low volume. I shook my head.

"I don't think it will kill me," I said.

She patted me on the back. "I thought his letter was lovely. You should be happy."

"Love is never happy. It is too busy suffering."

"If that is true, then there is no reason to get out of bed in the morning."

I tapped her on top of her head with the rose. "You're right, my friend. There is no reason to get up. Do you want to have some ice cream? If I cannot have the boy I love, I may as well get fat."

Maybe she hadn't heard exactly what I said.

Kabrina nodded. "Ice cream is our friend."

6

The months went by, and I hated them. The *Traveler* was an arrow flying toward a target drawn on my chest. When it struck that last percent of velocity, I felt the blood would pour from my finger. It was ironic. Even in our ultramodern world of antibiotics and every conceivable medical device, my thumb did become infected, as Kabrina had feared. And it wouldn't get better. The swelling was always there: a dull ache, an ugly color, nothing too serious, nothing really to complain about. But nothing that would go away either. Yet after a while I think I welcomed the infection. Somehow, to me, it meant my blood was no longer pure. That I had defiled it by choosing my duty over my love. It was a reminder of what I had both lost and thrown away.

Tem wrote me each month. His letters grew longer, more witty, more sentimental, while mine remained stunted bursts of melancholy. We were

still in almost normal time. Tem was still only two
years older than I was. But as I watched our
speedometer, I saw a reflection of a ghoul's calen-
dar. There was no red Santa Claus to commemo-
rate Christmas this year. Only a skull and
crossbones hanging over the last month of the year.
In one letter Tem said he was sending my Christmas present comet express—he had found such a
service, he said. And I wanted to believe him. I put
my infected finger to my head and squeezed my
temples so tight another drop of blood fell from my
thumb and ran like a vampire's tear over his
signature.

I couldn't bear it.

7

As the crucial ten days neared, the earth days when
Tem would grow old, die, and become dust, I went
to my father's quarters. It was not often I visited
him alone. We usually met in public places: for a
meal, to watch a show. This time I went without

notice, late, when I feared he might be sleeping. Yet I should have remembered how little rest he needed. He was sitting at a computer monitor when I walked in. He hardly looked up.

"Paige," he said. "This is a pleasant surprise."

I sat beside him at his desk. "Is it?" I asked.

He raised an eyebrow, but didn't stop working. "What's the matter? Don't you feel well?"

I considered. "I lied to you."

"About what?"

"My friend. Tem. Do you remember him?"

He frowned. "The boy you met before we left?"

"Yes. Him."

"What about him?"

"He's going to die."

My father turned off his computer and looked at me. "What's wrong with him?"

"Nothing." I gestured helplessly. "But he's going to die of old age. In the next month."

My father shook his head. "You knew that was inevitable when you boarded the ship."

"The fact that something is inevitable doesn't make it less painful." I paused. "Besides, it isn't inevitable."

"What are you talking about?" he asked.

"I want to go home. I want to return to earth. Before we move into ultra-time dilation. I want you to turn the ship around, begin to decelerate." I paused. "Please."

He stared at me, then sighed. "That's impossible."

"I knew you'd say that. But it isn't impossible. You're the captain. If you give the order, it will be done."

"You can't be serious, Paige."

"I am. I'm your daughter. You should know when I'm serious. You should know when I'm lying." A tear crept into my voice. "You should have known I was in love."

"You didn't tell me how much he meant to you."

My voice cracked. "You didn't ask! Oh, yeah, you wanted to know if I'd had a good time on my vacation. But you didn't really want to know what I did with that time. How precious it was to me—every second of it."

He moved to touch me, perhaps to wipe a tear from my face. But then seemed to think better of it. He had never seen this side of his daughter. I was always cool and professional around him. Maybe he was afraid I'd bite him. He withdrew his hand and sat silent for a minute.

"We have a responsibility," he said finally. "To the crew of this ship. To earth. To humanity. Never before has a past generation been able to see future generations as we will, to evaluate and advise them. Two centuries will bring us tremendous progress, but as a people we may lose something as well. We are mankind's guarantee that we lose nothing. Do you understand this?"

"I have heard all that before. But I don't understand it. Because I'm not mankind. No one is. We're all individuals. You have to treat me like an individual right now. Father, please, I'm the only family you've got. Not that I'm sure what that means to you. I know you loved my mother, but I don't know how you feel about me. But I can tell you how you *should* feel. I should be the most important thing in your life. More important than any mission. I—"

"Paige," he interrupted.

"I have never asked you for anything before in my life!" I continued. "But I'm asking you this. Turn this ship around. Let me go back to a time I know, not to an alien future that won't know me. Let me go back to him."

He took time to respond. "You know I can't do that."

"What if I beg you? What if I tell you that I can't live without him?"

"I can't." He lowered his head. "You'll get over it. Time—"

"Time!" I interrupted, standing. "Time will not heal this wound. Time is the enemy here." I paused. "What if I tell you—if you don't turn around the ship—I'll hate you for the rest of my life?"

He raised his head, met my eyes. "Will you, Paige?"

His gaze did something to me. I was staring into my own genetic code. But the family mirror was smeared with dust, fine particles that mysteriously settled with each passing moment, unseen by anyone until it was too late. I couldn't wipe them away by striking him, and besides the gesture would be as futile as it was improper. Yet I do know I hated him right then.

Already Tem was five years older than I was, not two.

I couldn't answer my father. There was no point. He wasn't going to help me. For that moment Tem died inside me. Many things did. I turned and left my father's quarters.

Tem's letters had piled up. They were in our computer banks, I knew, and I would have read them all at once except for my vow. That was all I had left as our November moved into December. The changing of the season—a cold wind would blow for sure. I could feel the winter dust of cometary tails already chapping the skin of my face.

But during those days, after confronting my father, I often thought of the last time we had been in space together. Two years earlier my father had been assigned to captain the *Questar* to go out to colonize another star system. It would have been a one-way mission. By the time we arrived at our destination—a system five hundred light years distant—over five centuries would have passed on earth. Yet aboard the *Questar* we would have been alive and going somewhere. At least when I was sixteen I didn't know Tem. I was looking forward to the adventure. A fresh start on a new world.

But we were barely out of the solar system when disaster struck. The *Questar* had a religious fanatic aboard who didn't believe it was God's will that mankind colonize other worlds. He worked in engineering and sabotaged the engines so that as we approached a velocity of ten million miles an hour, the graviton drive overloaded and we were in desperate danger of exploding. The man had perished completing his dirty work. When the graviton drives were on, they were not easily approached by a human being. Usually the person ended up being disrupted at a cellular level.

But to fix the damage and save our lives, someone had to get to the drives and repair them. A robotic probe couldn't do it; too many human decisions had to be made at the repair sight, and the gravity wave put off by the drive would disrupt communication with a robot. Therefore, a person had to go, a hero, and he had to go knowing he would not be coming back.

Of course my father wanted to do it. He was the

captain; it was his ship. And whatever qualities my father may have lacked, courage was not one of them. He was suiting up when his chief engineer managed to convince him that he, the engineer, was more qualified to do the repair. I was with my father then and I saw what it took out of him to send one of his best friends to his death. But the engineer was right. He was better equipped for the job, and my father knew that.

So we lived, and the engineer died. But our ship was already too damaged. We had to turn around and head for home. The loss of the mission hurt my father deeply. Yet he never complained, about it or anything else. I thought about that as I thought of the ultimatum I had given him. He was right—it was a foolish request. But, then, love is foolish. So I had damaged our relationship for nothing. There had never been a chance he would listen to me.

Besides thinking of my father, I often day-dreamed of Tem. I have said he was already dead to me, and that was true—I had given up all hope. But that didn't stop me from remembering our short time together. There had been one night in particular, when we had taken the ram jet to Hawaii—a thirty-minute flight—and scuba dived off Maui under the full moon. The reef was alive with fish and turtles and we stayed in the water half the night. When we finally returned to the shore we were so exhausted that we fell asleep on the sand. When the sun came up the next morning, it woke me before Tem. I remember how I leaned over and stared at his sleeping face and listened to his rhythmic breathing. I kissed his cheek and whispered in his ear.

"I'm going to see you again, after this week," I said. "I don't know how, but I will, Tem. I swear it. You're not getting away from me."

He just went right on sleeping.

Now I saw it was me who went right on dreaming.

9

Christmas Day I sat in the dimly lit viewing area and stared at the distant sun. I did not need a calculator to count the passing years. We were at our desired velocity—it was one year every hour. Tem was turning into a wrinkled old man before my eyes. Even if I couldn't see him.

This was the big time. Our graviton drive was off. All our instruments were aimed at earth, monitoring how society was changing. I was ignoring my job as a sociologist, but I knew I could always analyze the data later. If I ran to the control room it was even possible I'd receive a final message from Tem. He'd be in his nineties. But I had promised him I wouldn't cheat on our promise to each other. I could only read his last message—if there was one—when I was an old lady.

I sat in the control room all Christmas Day. Tem must have aged twenty-four years in the process. He must have died—my present from Santa.

My grief, that day, was terrible.

Yet I did not feel him die.

10

The week passed. By New Year another century had gone by. For some reason I got sick that week. I lay in my quarters and stared at the ceiling and burned with fever. Maybe it was my infected finger. I didn't care. My father visited me once, but I still had nothing to say to him.

I kept Tem's lock of hair pressed to my heart.

11

We had hardly begun to decelerate—our velocity was a fraction less than it had been Christmas Day—when we were attacked. We did not face the onslaught alone. Wave upon wave of black ships first assaulted the earth, then the lunar and Mars colonies. They came out of nowhere and were far more advanced technologically than those of humanity's. We were still experiencing time dilation, so we observed the entire battle on earth in less than an hour, although mankind did fight for several bitter days. The aliens had very powerful energy weapons and just wiped out humanity. Like they could have cared less. When they were finished, earth glowed with radioactive poison.

They sent only a small vessel after us.

They radioed ahead. They called themselves the Shamere and wanted us to surrender or else—they made it very clear—we would be destroyed.

I sat on the bridge with my father as the Shamere ship approached.

I don't think he even knew I was there, at first.

The alien vessel looked like a black thorn, tipped with blood.

My vision had not cleared since earth had been incinerated.

I was beyond tears. It was too much, by five billion lives.

"They didn't spare anyone else," my father said. "Why don't they just open fire on us and end it?"

"They may want to study our ship before they kill us," Number One—Kabrina's father—said. "Our ship is two hundred years older than anything they encountered over earth."

"They didn't study any of earth's ships," my father replied. "What else could they want?"

"Specimens," Number One said. "To study. To display. To dissect."

My father frowned. The *Traveler* was not heavily armed, so he didn't have a lot of options. We had a hundred antimatter missiles, two massive graviton disrupters—each of which was capable of pulverizing a large asteroid to dust. But from what we had seen of the battle over earth, our weapons would be smoke blowing against their protective shields. Nevertheless, my father didn't want to go down without a fight.

"Arm missiles," he ordered. "Lock on disrupters."

"Wait," I said.

My father glanced over at me. "You shouldn't be here."

"What does it matter if we're all about to die?" I stood and addressed my father and Number One. "Let them board us. They'll be less likely to blow us out of the sky with their own people in our midst."

"You assume they will board us," Number One said.

I shrugged. "We have nothing to lose."

My father considered. "I lean toward Number One's theories. It might be better to die than live and go through what they have planned for us."

"It's possible they know that we are a ship out of time," I said. "They might be curious about our past. They might not harm us."

"Curiosity does not appear to be a dominant trait in this race," Number One said. "They didn't even give earth a chance to surrender. They came in firing."

"But they are giving us a chance." I added, "It's better to decide for life than death."

My father stood up from his seat and strode to the large forward viewing screen. The Shamere vessel was within range of our weapons. Not that it mattered much, from the aliens' perspective. They were safe behind their impenetrable shields. My father stared hard at the alien vessel. He looked old right then.

"Signal them that we surrender," he said finally.

"Captain!" Number One said, shocked.

My father raised his hand. "We can *appear* to surrender. It might buy us time."

"To do what?" Number One asked.

"To search for weaknesses," my father answered. "To find an opening. To attack." He glanced at me. He had appreciated my earlier comments. He didn't have to say so for me to know. "Give me another idea of what they might want from us?"

I, too, stared at the approaching ship. Somehow, it reminded me of my infected finger. It was as if the aliens were a virus in the body of humanity. Yet that made no sense because they had for all practical purposes just lopped off the host body's head.

But something about the approaching ship seemed familiar.

I frowned. "I think they are personally interested in us. Don't ask me why. It's just a feeling I get."

12

The Shamere accepted our surrender, on the surface. They sent an order that they would indeed be boarding, and that all but the captain of our ship was to go to his or her quarters. The Shamere said that anyone who was not in quarters would be executed on sight. My father told everyone, including myself, to comply, but I refused to obey. This angered my father. He paced uneasily as we waited on the bridge for the Shamere to reach us. Six of them had already entered our aft airlock. I had only caught a glimpse of them in the monitors. Although humanoid in shape, they were ugly critters.

"Paige," my father said. "If we know nothing else about these aliens, we know they are murderers. You have to get out of here."

"I'm not afraid of them."

"That doesn't matter. They'll kill you."

"They're probably going to kill all of us anyway."

He stopped pacing. "I could have you thrown out of here."

"You would have to do it yourself." I paused. "I think you need me by your side. I make better decisions than you."

He smiled, despite his anger. "Your mother used to say that."

"I am my mother's daughter." I paused. "And my father's." I caught his eye. "I am sorry. My demand was unworthy. It was just that I . . . I was in so much pain."

"I accept your apology." He studied me. "How are you now?"

I shrugged and gestured in the direction of our dead earth. "My individual feelings seem unimportant right now. Do you think the Shamere know about our star colonies?"

"Probably. They could all be wiped out already."

I had to put a hand to my head. "So this is it? Humanity is finished?"

"It doesn't look good, Paige."

I nodded weakly. "How about earth? How long will she be radioactive?"

"Millions of years. All life has been destroyed there, down to the tiniest virus."

"Could it return? Is it possible?"

He sighed. "I honestly don't know." He pointed to a lit purple button on the compact control panel attached to the arm of his command chair. "I have rigged the ship to explode. If for some reason I can't get to that button, and the situation looks bad, you—"

"I understand," I interrupted. I glanced at the monitors, studying the Shamere as they hurried through our corridors. Without being given directions, they knew where our bridge was. That puzzled me. It was not easily spotted from the outside.

The Shamere had large heads, shrunken bodies. Their skin was a ghastly white, terribly wrinkled. They moved with effort, unnaturally, as if it took all their energy to balance their heads on their scrawny necks and torsos. They had large slobbery mouths, massive solid-blue eyes that glistened with a cold light. They wore gold-colored space suits, and carried deadly looking energy weapons. They moved surprisingly fast for short-limbed creatures.

"What do you think of them?" my father asked.

"They look cruel and smart," I said. "A bad combination."

My father nodded. "I have to say it again. You may have only a minute left to live. They said they would execute the first person who disobeyed them."

I forced a smile. "I'll try to charm them with my good looks and biting wit." I paused. "My life has been good. I have no regrets."

"I know that's not true, and that I am responsible for many things you were not able to do. But I'm happy, at least, that you knew love once in your life."

His words touched me deeply. "I knew it twice, silly. Remember, I met you first."

He, too, seemed moved by my comment. He reached over and squeezed my hand. Nothing like the end of the world to bring a father and daughter together, and I don't mean that cynically. Our conversation would never have taken place without the absolute horror of the situation.

My father and I stood as they neared our door. I had the lock of Tem's hair pinned inside my uniform, near my heart.

The door opened and the monsters poured in.

The six entered together. One wore a green jewel on his suit. He appeared to be the leader. He had more hair than the rest; a red stubble on top of a wrinkled white skull. He gestured with his weapon to my father and spoke in passable English, in a voice thick with mucus and arrogance. Where had he learned? Perhaps the aliens had been observing us for years before their attack.

"You are the captain of this vessel?" he asked.

"Yes." My father stepped forward and offered his hand. "I'm Captain Karl Christian. This is my daughter, Paige Christian."

The Shamere did not accept my father's hand. His hard eyes were on me. The rest of the Shamere had fanned out around us. They held their weapons ready, not exactly trusting types.

"What is she doing here?" the leader demanded.

"I help him run this ship," I said. "He would be lost without me."

THE STARLIGHT CRYSTAL

"She is my First Officer," my father said quickly. "I assumed you would want to speak to both of us."

The Shamere leader took a step toward me, eyeing me up and down. He had bad breath; it smelled as if he had just eaten a small child. He would be capable of it, I knew. His expression was hard to fathom, but he obviously did not like me. He poked my ribs with the muzzle of his weapon.

"You are no First Officer," he said. "You are a child."

I pushed aside his weapon. "And you are a guest aboard this ship. Where are your manners?"

The Shamere leader glanced at his partners. He slowly grinned—a disgusting gesture—and they grinned with him. They all slobbered on the breasts of their gold suits.

"You are as our records show," he said in his nauseating voice. "Intellectually inferior and psychologically unstable."

I snorted. "I'd rather have a lower IQ than have a fat head like yours."

My father stepped between us, clearly worried that I was about to be eviscerated in front of him. "Perhaps the Shamere leader would like to discuss the terms of surrender?" he said hastily.

The alien leader's big blue eyes continued to linger on me. But his grin had faded. "There are no terms. You are our prisoners. You will order your crew to begin boarding our ship immediately."

My father was not pleased. Slowly, he moved in the direction of his command chair and the purple

41

button. It was only three steps away; he had stayed intentionally close to it.

"That's not acceptable," he said. "Before my people move to your ship, I must have a guarantee that they will be treated properly as prisoners of war."

The Shamere leader pointed his weapon at my father's chest. "Your people will be treated as any inferior species is. With scorn and contempt."

My father's eyes flashed on the purple button, back to the Shamere commander. "Why do you have such contempt for us?" he asked. "What did we ever do to you?"

The alien's expression was hateful. "It disgusts us to know you still live."

"Still?" I said. "Has our race encountered yours before?"

The alien group grinned as a whole. Except for the commander. His hate only deepened. He approached me once more. Already it was decided between my father and me. Things were as bad as they could get. My father had to reach that button. Better we die with dignity, I thought, and take a few of these monsters with us. The leader put a smelly hand on my shoulder and stared into my eyes. It took all my will power to meet his gaze. Finally, I felt the terror of what we were up against. In that moment I heard the screams of the billions who had perished on earth. They echoed in the dark part of my soul.

"You do not know who we are, do you?" he said. "You do not know where we come from."

"I'm curious about your origin," I said, straining to keep my voice even. "I would be happy to listen to a description of your home world."

That caused the group to laugh. The leader even smiled, but it was a cold gesture. He brushed my hair aside with the tip of one of his slimy fingers.

"You would not be happy, Paige," the leader said. And it was only then that I realized that the alien was a female. I don't know how I knew it—maybe it was something in the voice. Certainly there was power in her tone. It was hypnotic and pushed me into portions of my mind that I did not consciously wish to enter. Yet it wasn't as if I flashed on traumatic memories. The present moment was more horrible than anything I could dredge up from the past. But as the alien stared at me, I thought of the woman who had steered me in the direction of Rainbow Park a week before we left earth. The person who, in a sense, had led me to Tem.

The Shamere leader reminded me of this woman. Curious.

I gathered my strength and sneered. "You know, the more you talk, the more inferior you sound. You have your powerful energy beams, sure, and your impenetrable shields. But you have no breeding. It doesn't matter that you've wiped us out. Some higher race will come along soon and smash your ugly faces into the dirty end of the Milky Way. Oh, and get your slimy hand off me." I pushed the alien's finger aside. "You're messing up my uniform." I paused and spoke softly, still holding the alien's eye. "Father."

My father leapt for the purple button.

The Shamere leader's reflexes were extraordinary.

In a flash she turned and leveled her weapon at my father's midsection. There was a burst of blue light, followed by an explosion of red. My face was splattered with hot blood and gross tissue. I turned away in horror, but not before I saw enough to know that my father was no more. I felt a strong hand grab my arm, a hard weapon put to my ear.

"Take this one to my ship now," the Shamere leader said. "We will open her up, and see why she is the way she is."

13

The alien who grabbed me, however, did not lead me to one of the *Traveler*'s airlocks. Instead he took me back into the engineering section, down into the bowels of the graviton drive, where few of us ever ventured, even when the power was off. Now the engines were on full; their throbbing displacement waves and full spectrum emissions overwhelmed my already deranged senses. My hair stood on end and my eyes rapidly blinked as we hurried down a long hallway that directly overlooked the energy center of the *Traveler*.

But still soaked with my father's blood and numbed by the suddenness of his death, I hardly cared where we were going. We were doomed. I saw no hope anywhere. I just wanted a quick shot to my head. I just wanted the pain to stop, for there to be nothing. No earth, no Paige, no father, no Tem. Oblivion; I longed to touch it.

This alien, though, stopped and spoke to me. He

had released my arm and was no longer pointing his weapon in my face.

"This vessel cannot fight a Shamere warship," he said. "The highest level of human technology is presently two levels below that of our own. There is no hope in staying here, in this time, and fighting us." He shook me with his slimy hands. "Do you understand?"

"Sure do," I mumbled. "Who cares?"

He spoke with urgency. "You must care, Paige Christian. You do not understand what has happened to your people. You do not understand why it had to happen. But that understanding is not for now. It will come in the eons to follow. You must go on. This ship and your friends must survive."

I rubbed my eyes and tried to get a fix on him. "Are you a good alien or what? Why are you telling me these things?"

In response he pulled a large glowing emerald crystal from his suit pocket. The thing was as bright as the graviton engines. I had to shield my eyes from it, although the light was fascinating in its richness of color and the rhythm with which it pulsed.

"This is a source of great power," he said. "I am going to infuse it into the plasma stream of your graviton drive. I am familiar with your propulsion systems. The elements are compatible, and there will be no explosion. Your drive will immediately displace a gravity wave a thousand times what this vessel normally does. That will boost your speed so close to that of light that time will lose all meaning aboard this vessel. But from the Shamere ship's point of view, it will be as if you disappeared. Do you understand?"

I was beginning to. This ugly duck was offering us a way out. Why?

"If we displace that much gravity," I said, "we won't be able to decelerate without a similar displacement." I nodded to the green crystal. "Do you have any extras?"

"Yes." He turned. "I will give them to you in a moment. But right now I must boost the plasma. There is not much time. Stay here while I move to the core opening. You will be safe here. The radiation will not harm you."

I grabbed his arm. "Why are you helping us?"

He held my eye a moment. Once again, I had a feeling of power, a dizzying moment of déjà vu. But this time I sensed love. I didn't doubt this creature.

"You will understand when you need to understand," he said. "The pattern is already established. The vector converges—it has to be this way."

"But," I began.

But he was gone, into the elevator that would take him down into regions of the graviton drive that humans did not dare enter without heavy protection. It occurred to me then, as I waited for him to reach the plasma stream, that when he displaced the gravity wave, he would have no way to get back to his ship. Time would fly at a miraculous rate. His ship would only exist in the past.

I could see the alien down below as he emerged from the elevator. We were separated by a transparent barrier that absorbed the majority of the harmful radiations that the engines emitted. But he was on the other side of the barrier. He was still flesh and blood, even if the particulars of his physiology were different from mine. I did not believe he would survive the operation on our drive.

He waved to me as he moved toward the plasma stream.

I saw him open the core and place the crystal inside.

The engines went insane. The noise was deafening, the light blinding. I did not physically feel the acceleration, of course—the pressure of it would have crushed me if it had been allowed to affect the interior of the ship. But I sensed our velocity. Outside, I could feel the stars age. I did not have to see them.

In the midst of it all, I saw a shadow run toward me down the long corridor the friendly alien had just dragged me. It was the Shamere leader, who held her weapon in front of her like a bayonet. Before I could even get off a warning shout, the leader had her weapon raised and was taking aim at her partner. In the effulgent storm a blue beam carved down from our precarious ledge. The death beam tore through a portion of the protective barrier. It burned into the friendly alien's chest. It destroyed the extra emeralds he carried in his pockets. Yet these did not explode. They simply died with their owner.

Two bloody deaths in succession. I couldn't even cry.

The Shamere leader pointed her weapon at me.

She smiled. Murder was her pleasure.

Then she erupted in red flame as a laser tore into her back.

Her howls echoed, mingling with the screams of the graviton drive.

She toppled in a messy lump. She smoked; she stank.

Number One and his daughter, Kabrina, ran to my side.

"Are you all right?" Kabrina cried.

I hugged her. "Yes. But where are the other aliens?"

Number One holstered his laser. "We killed them. Not all of us sat quietly in our quarters." He paused. "Your father . . ."

"He's dead," I whispered.

Kabrina held on to me. "We know."

"But what about the Shamere warship?" I asked.

We had to return to the bridge to answer that question.

As my alien had promised, we had escaped. The warship was in the past. We were at ninety-nine-point-nine-nine-nine-nine-nine-nine-nine-

nine—the nines went on forever—the speed of light. The chronometer spun madly. Every second that went by aboard our ship—a thousand years went by outside. We were not even allowed to savor the miracle of our release. If we could not stop ourselves, somehow slow our speed, there would be no time for anything, joys or sorrows.

The entire universe would simply run out of time.

14

Several of our days had elapsed since our encounter with the Shamere. We had cremated the dead—a shocking total of twenty-eight. The Shamere soldiers had not gone down without a fight, killing many of the crew. The aliens we had also burned, in the fires of our engines, except for the commander's body. It was put into cold storage, for future examination. But the ashes of my father and the five monsters trailing behind us merged in a long tail as cold as it was dark. Starlight, stardust . . . I think I may, I think I must.

I missed my father a great deal.

I missed Tem. Always.

I sat in the observation deck and stared at the earth through our main telescope, which was capable of picking out minute details on the planet even from this distance. Many millions of years had elapsed since the devastating attack. Finally the radiation had ceased to glow. Yet, even though the oceans were as blue as ever, the puffy clouds white, there was no hint of green on the land. The Shamere had burned the seeds of all future gestation. The earth was barren.

In my hand I had a printout from my personal computer file.

Tem's seventh letter.

Paige,

By the time you get this letter, I'll probably be dead. For that reason, this letter is particularly hard to write. Almost, I hear the funeral organ playing mournfully behind you, and I want to say something to comfort you. I am torn between describing how rich life is on earth, and how miserable I am without you.

But I will do neither. I will say what I can. I was not asleep that morning in Hawaii, when we lay on the beach together. I heard what you whispered to me, about how I wasn't getting away from you. Paige, I need to tell you this. I hope a part of you understands.

You were right.

Your eternal friend,
Tem

According to my promise, I was supposed to write him back. But I didn't know what to say to a ghost who had been sure he would never die. I felt like the spirit then, set adrift in an uncaring universe where there were everlasting souls, but no God. I thought of God as I held the letter and stared at the earth. I wondered, in all that had happened, where he could be. I wondered *how* he could be, to exist and yet allow the Shamere to destroy our world. The stars had shifted dramatically since we'd departed. Some had already begun to dim. The old constellations were gone, the ancient myths forgotten. My faith in God was in shambles.

But maybe he knew that.

15

I was in the garden the following day with Kabrina when it started. Once again, we were pruning the rose bushes. I was careful of the thorns; my right thumb continued to fester with its mild infection. I had let the doctors treat it but their medicines had no effect. Not that it mattered now. We were talking about Tem's letter.

"But you must write him back," Kabrina said. "That's the point of it all. That you keep your relationship alive in your heart. That's why he made you promise him to write."

"I know that," I replied, facing her so that she could understand me. "I suppose I will write him. I just feel stupid trying to send the letter to him. You know, I have to go up to the bridge and hand it to the communication officer on duty and tell him or her, 'Yeah, it's a letter for my dead boyfriend. Can you be sure to get it off this afternoon?'" I shook my head. "All the other letters I sent, at least Tem was alive then."

"No love is ever lost," Kabrina said casually. Then she paused and her eyes seemed to sparkle, for an instant. Standing rock still, she spoke in an exceptionally clear voice. "Love is eternal. It is the very matter of the Creation."

I glanced over. "That's very poetic."

"Yes." Then she became still again, and once more her voice was clearer than usual. "Poetry is the language of the soul. Silence is the song."

I smiled. "You're in a philosophical mood."

Kabrina appeared puzzled. "There's something here."

"What?"

"There's a presence here."

I set down my shears and stepped to her side. "What are you talking about?"

She stared at me with unfocused eyes. "I feel something wants to communicate with us."

She was making me nervous. "You're kidding?"

"No. I feel it. Don't you feel it?"

The truth is I did feel something, some presence. *Presence* was an apt word; this "thing" definitely was not physical, even though the hairs on the back of my head tingled with electricity. It was as if a wave had swept over me. There was a lightness in the air, an unlooked for joy. Kabrina slowly sat on the grass, as if pressed down by invisible fingers. I knelt beside her as she closed her eyes.

"Ask me questions," she said.

Kabrina was deaf. If I asked, and her eyes were closed, she would know nothing. I touched her arm to indicate the trouble, but she shook me off.

"Ask," she said, her voice still much clearer than usual. "Don't worry about the ears."

I drew in a shaky breath. "Can you hear me?"

"Not with the ears. But we hear you."

I gasped. "Oh God."

"That could be a word for what we are, but it is not a word we prefer. It means too many things to different people. Call us the Creation. We are one with it, as you are. The only difference is we realize that, and you do not."

"Kabrina!" I exclaimed.

"What?"

"Why are you saying these things? How can you hear me?"

Kabrina frowned. "I cannot hear you. But I know what you are saying."

"How?"

"This presence knows. Let's just talk to it for a moment, and see what it has to say."

"But does it put you in a trance?"

"No." Then her voice grew stronger. Kabrina had switched gears. She was no longer speaking; at least the thoughts expressed were not her own. "This is higher telepathy. No trance is required. This individual is able to communicate with us directly. This individual will is not compromised. There is no danger. In fact, for her to be with us, enriches both of you." A pause. "You feel better?"

I did feel better. More energetic, yet calmer.

"Yes," I said. "Who are you?"

"We are not individual as you understand individuality. Yet we have individual qualities. A wave rises on an ocean. For a time, it can be seen. It is still the ocean and yet it is separate from it as well. This communication is like that. Individuality is assumed for the sake of this relationship. Yet it is in reality the ocean of Creation that speaks to you."

"Why? Why speak to us?"

"We are bound to you with a thread of love. This relationship exists only because of love. Indeed, the Creation is nothing but love."

"I can't believe this is happening," I muttered. "Kabrina, you must be joking with me."

"She does not hear with physical senses. She hears with her heart. Feel with your heart and you will know this communication is genuine." A pause. "What do you feel, Paige Christian?"

My eyes were damp, and I struggled with the warmth that continued to grow inside my chest. "Gratitude."

"Very good. Grace flows where there is gratitude. That is why the words are similar. Grace is the love of the Creation for the created. Grace is the essence of our relationship with you. We are here to serve."

"But who are you? Are you alien beings?"

"No. We are the same as you. We are the Creation, you are the Creation. We are all things. But once, we were like you in the sense that once we did not know we were the Creation. We were thirsty fish swimming in an ocean, searching for a drink. Where is the ocean? we would say to ourselves. We had heard so much about it. We even built temples to people whom we believed had once seen the ocean. We turned them into prophets, then we fought amongst ourselves over which prophet was right and which was wrong." A pause. "You are that fish. You exist in an ocean of joy and yet your sorrow reaches even to us. Tell us, why are you so sad?"

"But you must know. You seem to know everything about us."

"We know. We understand. We are here to give you understanding, if you desire it. What is it you desire, Paige Christian?"

I had to lower my head. "You mean, what do I wish for most of all?"

"Yes."

I shrugged. "There was this guy I once knew. I would give anything to see him again." I stopped. "But I'll never see him. He's dead."

"This is Tem?"

"Yes. You know of him?"

"Yes."

I struggled. "What can you tell me about him?"

"It is better we talk of you than him, of your desire to see him. Do you want to hear a deep secret?"

"Yes."

"What you most wish for, what you most hope for—that is your greatest illusion. The greatest barrier that separates you from the Creation." A pause. "We understand this idea will be controversial. People say hold on to your dreams, wish upon the brightest star, and that is fine at a certain point along the path. You struggle to accomplish your dreams—it seems they never come true unless you struggle. But then the night slowly begins to fade. The light of day begins to dawn. The time for dreaming passes. It is then you must leave them behind." A pause. "You cannot know true joy when you are bound by desire. It is not possible."

I struggled to respond. The concepts were overwhelming. They hit me like waves crashing upon rocks. I felt a lump in my throat as I tried to explain about Tem.

"I didn't ask to love him," I said. "I just do. But I don't want to give up this love. You say love is all there is. I feel it is all I have left of him, my feelings for him."

"We understand. Yet you cannot see the true light of the Creation while you wear dark glasses of illusion. Tem is not dead. There is no death. Only the form has changed. The essence remains as it always was—a wave dissolving into the ocean."

"I wish I could believe that."

"Another wish, Paige Christian? You can trust us. We are fishermen. We know when to throw out our nets, when to draw them back in. We are drawn to you." A pause. "Tem is happy."

"I hope so." I swallowed before continuing. "You

must know our predicament. We are stranded in space and time. We can't slow down. All around us, the universe is running down. If we don't stop soon, we fear it will all be over." I added, "We're so alone out here."

"You are not alone. We are here. Others of your kind are also around."

My hand flew to my mouth. "You mean there are other survivors of humanity?"

"Yes."

"Other star systems survived?"

"The ones we speak of are much closer than another star."

"Where are they?" I asked.

"Look and you will find them."

I trembled with excitement. Why? It was just a voice speaking, speaking with my best friend's vocal cords. Yet I knew in my heart it was much more than that. There was power in the words. There was love in the silence that vibrated between the sentences.

"I will have to think about what you have said," I replied. "Whoever you are."

"Think for seven of your days. It is then we will return. Hopefully, by then, all your people will gather to hear what we have to say."

"I don't think anyone will gather. I don't think anyone would believe this story, other than Kabrina and myself."

"You will be surprised then."

16

Seven days later the entire crew of the *Traveler* was gathered in the garden to hear the Creation speak through Kabrina. My best friend was hooked up to a microphone and a speaker system, although I sat at her knee on the grass and would be able to hear the words as they came out of her mouth. The others had come because already one of the predictions of the Creation had come true.

We were not alone. Maybe.

After our cosmic encounter, Kabrina and I had rushed to see her father. Of course he didn't believe a word of our story, especially since Kabrina was unable to duplicate her newfound hearing ability. Number One saw it as nothing more than an elaborate prank, even though Kabrina was not known as a joker.

"But I didn't plan any of this," Kabrina said. "I was just standing in the garden when I felt a wave of energy sweep over me. It was peaceful but powerful. Then, when I closed my eyes, I just knew what Paige was asking me."

Number One smiled. "She was asking *you*. You're both old enough not to be indulging in fantasies. There was no one else there. There couldn't be."

"But her eyes were closed," I insisted. "And the words were unlike anything Kabrina would say. Even her voice was clearer."

Number One lost his smile and shook his head. "Listen to yourselves. You're essentially saying that God wants to help us. Well, there is no God. The only help we're going to get is from ourselves."

"They never said they were God," I protested.

Kabrina lowered her head in disappointment. "I wouldn't lie to you, Father. Not about something like this."

"I'm not calling you a liar," Number One said.

"When I used to come to my father with a difficult proposition," I said, "he would often scoff at me. But at least he would check it out, to see if there was even a one-in-a-thousand chance that I might be right." I paused. "You're our captain now. What are you going to do?"

He regarded me critically, then sighed. "I suppose I could go into the monitor records to see what my daughter said and how she said it."

I nodded. "You'll be impressed."

17

Number One was puzzled after studying the recording. He could see on the tapes that Kabrina had been sitting with her eyes closed when I questioned her.

"Did you two set this up ahead of time?" he demanded.

"No," we both said.

"Well, what am I supposed to do with this information?" he asked.

"We should look for another ship," I said.

"Where? Out here? That's ridiculous."

"Why?" I asked. "Earth could have launched another ship into a time dilation. Why do we have to be the only one."

"They may have launched another ship. Another one was planned."

I gasped. "My father never said anything about that."

"It was classified as sensitive information,"

Number One said. "He wasn't permitted to talk about it, nor was I. It doesn't matter anyway. The Shamere surely destroyed the vessel, if it did exist."

"How can you say *surely* when we escaped destruction?" I asked. "Perhaps a friendly alien helped this other ship as well."

Number One shook his head. "Assuming there was another ship—it was only in the planning stages. Assuming the Shamere did help it somehow —it probably won't exist now. We were accelerated into this insane time dilation by sheer chance. I'm sure the Shamere who helped us meant to take us out of it immediately. I don't know if either of you has properly grasped how much time has elapsed in the normal universe since that battle. If there was another ship, if it did escape destruction, it would be gone now. There would be no point in contacting it."

"Our velocity is still high, but we are no longer accelerating," I said. "Our instruments are unobstructed. We have nothing else to do out here. We may as well search for it."

"Because some kind of super beings talking through my daughter says we should?" he asked with a trace of sarcasm.

"You forget, Father," Kabrina said. "They didn't tell us we had to do anything. They just gave us the information." She paused. "I don't think they would have told us that if our people were all dead."

18

Seek and you shall find. The spirits had spoken. But it was not that easy. We were traveling ridiculously fast. Every day, from an *outsider's* perspective, we circled the solar system thousands of times. Our mass was that of a giant sun. If anything lay in our path—comets or asteroids or the remains of once living worlds—it was obliterated. But space is bigger than the human mind can comprehend, vaster than mortal imagination can visualize. We did not have to worry about hitting something. But we did have to strain to find something. Particularly if it was only circling the solar system a few dozen times a year. Number One explained this to us on the bridge after he had completed a detailed scan of the immediate vicinity.

"Our instruments are not distorted due to the functioning of our drive," he said. "But they are greatly handicapped by our speed. We fly out of an area almost the instant we try to obtain a sensor reading." He consulted his monitors. "The cometary cloud still exists. There are many ship-size objects following a similar orbit to ours, but there is no way we will be able to examine any of those objects close enough to see if one's artificial."

An idea occurred to me. "You're using only sensors to find it?"

"Of course," Number One said. "What else would we use?"

"How about the radio?" I asked.

He smiled and spoke in a condescending tone. "We constantly monitor all known radio bands, Paige. That is standard procedure."

"I know that," I said. "But radio sent at what frequency? I mean, rather, at what rate of time dilation? This other ship could be experiencing one tenth our time distortion, or one millionth. We have to adjust our instruments, have them scan through each possible level of velocity. They could be trying to contact us now, but their message might be a thousand times too slow for us to pick up."

Number One was impressed. "An interesting suggestion. But such a scan, through millions of possible time dilation scenarios, would take time, even for our computers."

"We have time," I protested.

Number One shook his head and pointed to the main viewing screen. The sun had dimmed and taken on a faint reddish hue.

"It has begun to expand," he said.

"You mean it has begun to die?" I asked. That the sun, *our* sun, could perish did not seem possible.

"Yes," Number One said. "Still, throughout the Milky Way, new stars are being born. But not many. And the old ones, like our sun, are fading fast." He paused. "Time is the one thing we don't have in abundance."

Nevertheless, he initiated the scan.

19

On the seventh day, the supposed number of days it had taken God to create the universe, we made contact. The signal was simple—"Hello, is anyone there?" It repeated at hourly intervals—to us. It was probably being sent out every microsecond. We lowered the speed of our message several thousandfold and beamed a reply. But we got no response. The message was clearly automated.

The news of it swept through the *Traveler*.

But it was bittersweet news.

"Their ship is intact," Number One said. "But they must all be dead."

"I don't think we can make that assumption," I said.

"Can we make another?" Number One asked. "Clearly this other vessel, wherever it is, has only a fraction of our time dilation. That being the case, the occupants must have already experienced thousands of years since the Shamere attack."

"But there were extensive experiments being done on artificial hibernation when we left earth," I said. "It's possible this new ship used that technique. Its crew might be frozen."

"When we left earth, no frozen human had ever been successfully revived," Number One said.

"But they were getting close," I said.

"Why do you persist with this unlikely scenario?" he asked.

Kabrina spoke. "You considered it unlikely that there was another ship out here, yet the beings we spoke to predicted it. These same beings implied the people aboard were still alive. That is why Paige persists in being illogical—she has faith." Kabrina paused. "Do you, Father? They said they would return today. Don't you want to hear what they have to say?"

Number One considered. He reached for a button that would broadcast a message throughout the entire vessel.

"I will inform the crew we have visitors," he said.

20

So we sat in the garden and waited for the highly evolved beings who were one with the Creation to speak to us. Kabrina sipped from a glass of water before closing her eyes and taking several deep breaths. I had to wonder, with so many people gathered, what would happen if nothing happened. But my fears proved groundless. Moments before Kabrina said a word, the feeling of presence returned. It swept like a hush through the scattered audience, and I heard muttered sounds of awe.

"We come in love and peace," they said through Kabrina. "We are the silent ones, the old ones. We came before you, and we will come after. Our home is a world circling the most distant star, and also a place only an inch from the tip of your nose. We see through your senses, although we have none of our own. We are not physical beings, as you are, but we were once physical. We lived and died, we loved and cried. Therefore, we know you, we understand you." A pause. "We are here to serve you."

Number One did not sit far from his daughter. "Is it all right to ask questions?" he questioned.

"Yes. Ask what you will."

Another stir went through the crowd. Everybody knew of Kabrina's deafness. Number One had seen her hear on the tape, but it was quite different in person.

"How can we prove your reality to ourselves?" Number One asked.

"Proof is a quality demanded by the intellect. The heart does not require it. The heart knows, it feels the truth. What do you feel as we speak?"

"Confused," Number One admitted.

"Confusion is the beginning of knowing. Certainty is the bane of wisdom. You must know that you do not know, before you can learn. What would you like to learn from us?"

"Are the people aboard the ship we have detected still alive?"

"Yes."

"Are they in deep hibernation?"

"Yes."

Number One had to take a breath. Already he was falling under the power of the unseen presence. I understood exactly how he felt. The truth of the beings' words was hard to reject. They simply sounded as if they knew what they were talking about, and it had little to do with the information they conveyed, although that was fascinating in and of itself. There was conviction in the air—for believers and nonbelievers alike. Yet that was not to say Number One had set aside his intellect.

"You understand we have no way of reaching them unless we can slow down?" he asked.

"Yes."

"Can you tell us how to do that?" Number One said.

"You already have the means. It was in front of you all the time. What do you need to slow this ship?"

"The power to counteract the acceleration achieved by the Shamere's green crystal," Number One said.

"You need another one of these crystals?"

"Yes. But we don't know where to get one, or how to build one."

"The knowledge is contained in the cells of the Shamere you keep frozen in your laboratory. Clone her cells—you possess the technology. Grow a new alien commander, then ask her how to build a crystal. She will tell you how it is done."

I noted that they referred to the alien as female, just as I had suspected.

"There are two difficulties with that plan," Number One said. "It will take us years to grow a suitable clone, and we don't have much time at the rate the universe is running down. Also, we have no way of triggering the clone's original memories."

"You can grow the clone in a laboratory fired

from this vessel into a lower time dilation velocity. You have the power to accomplish this, and the power to recover the said laboratory. The clone will return to you fully grown, while only a few days will have passed."

Number One was impressed but cautious. "Everything would have to go perfectly for us to recover the laboratory."

"You must plan very carefully."

"But what of my second objection? How do we recover the original's memories from the clone?"

"Paige Christian will help."

I sat up, startled. "What can I do?"

"We will do it through you. If you hold the clone, it will talk through you."

"I'm sorry," Number One said. "You confuse us."

"We will explain." A pause. "We speak through the nervous system of this young woman, whom you call Kabrina. She is an excellent receiver for what we wish to convey. Even so, she cannot express everything we wish because there are natural limitations in her brain, in her knowledge of the Creation. We can take a simple example to illustrate this point. If we wish to use a word she does not know, we must chose another word." A pause. "We know how to build the green crystal for you, but none of you possess the requisite knowledge of physics and chemistry and biology for us to be able to convey the details of the crystal construction.

Therefore, we need the clone of the Shamere commander. In that alien nervous system is present all the requisite knowledge."

"Yet you said the clone will talk through Paige," Number One said. "Why through her?"

"You will see that she is the one. At this time, it is not permitted for us to explain why it has to be her." A pause. "We will return when the clone is ready. But you may continue to question us now."

"Who does not permit you?" Number One asked. "Do you have a higher authority above you?"

"No. We *are* the Creation. For us, there is no possibility of hierarchy." A pause. "We speak out of our own nature. We do not permit ourselves to reveal the answer to why Paige Christian will be able to speak for the Shamere clone once it has been grown. But we can say the experiment will succeed if you do everything possible to make it a success."

"Could the experiment fail?" Number One asked.

"Of course. It is possible. It is up to you."

"Why did one of the Shamere try to help us?" Number One asked.

"The answer to that question will also be revealed over time."

"We will know the answer once we have cloned the Shamere commander?"

"Paige Christian will know the answer when it is time. Others will not know."

"Why her again?" Number One asked.

"It is her destiny."

"Is there destiny?" Number One asked. "Or is there free will?"

"Along the path there is free will. Once the goal is reached the understanding dawns that everything was destined. But a man or a woman cannot pretend to be at the goal while still on the path. At this time you must act as if you have free will."

"But in reality it does not exist?" Number One asked.

"In our reality it does not exist. In your reality it does exist. Still, in your reality there is destiny. Paige Christian has a unique destiny. All aboard this ship do. It will unfold in time, if you have the courage to allow it."

"You speak of a path," Number One said. "Where does this path lead?"

"To the Creation."

"But we are already in the Creation," Number One said.

"Yes, but you are also separate from it. You keep yourselves separate from it. But we do not blame you. The parents understand the ways of the child. But it is the parents' responsibility to teach the child."

"Will you teach us to become one with the Creation?" Number One asked.

"Yes. It is why we are here. To serve."

"How long will it take us to become one with the Creation?"

"Time has no meaning on the path. The goal can be reached in an instant, or it can take billions of years to achieve. Each goes at his or her own speed. But each must travel the same path, although it may seem to take many forms. There are seven stops along the road. We will outline them once you have begun to decelerate, and have begun to reenter normal time."

"Why then?" Number One asked.

"Because only then will our instruction have value for you. Understand this point and do not become agitated—the Creation has gone forward while you have stood still. You are seeds that never saw the harvest. We are the farmers. We remember where each seed was planted. But once, we were also seeds. We know what it is like to be hidden in the dark, deprived of the nourishing light of the sun. We know your pain, and we know your capacity for joy. For us, that joy can light up the entire Creation."

"Even as it dies?" Number One asked.

"You will see. You will be amazed."

21

"Will she look as ugly as before?" I asked Number One as he prepared to jettison the pod that would grow the Shamere commander. The pod was black and small, only ten feet long and half that in diameter. It looked like a coffin, not a nursery. The shuttle it was being fitted into was ten times that size. It was the shuttle's job to knock even a millionth of a point off our virtual speed of light velocity. That would allow time aboard the shuttle to accelerate, and our dear alien would be fully grown in a week. I still didn't see how I was going to help the Creation get into the monster's mind. I just hoped I didn't have to touch the alien.

"She will look exactly as she did before," Number One said. He prepared to close the pod. "Do you want to say goodbye?"

The interior of the pod was fitted with an artificial womb. At present the Shamere commander was a handful of cells reproducing inside a flexible test tube. The ruined body of the commander was still in cold storage. We had swiped only a few of its reproductive cells, for the cloning process.

Its DNA was not unlike our own.

"I want to say good riddance," I said.

Number One smiled and closed the pod. "According to our super beings, this alien is our only chance of survival."

"So you call them super beings? It's funny they never gave us a name other than telling us to call them the Creation."

"Perhaps they will tell us next time."

I touched Number One's arm. Even though I continued to argue with him over everything we did, my respect for him had grown. No one could replace my father, but the crew looked up to Kabrina's father, and they trusted him. I did as well.

"Do you believe this will work?" I asked. "Really?"

He was thoughtful. "I was studying the earth through our main telescope today. Did you know the oceans are gone?"

I felt a stab of pain. "No. Will they return?"

"No. The sun continues to swell. All the water has been burned off as vapor into space. Earth will never have oceans again. It's brown and desolate looking. The clouds are gone as well. But I don't bring that up to depress you. Your question reminds me of how I felt staring at our world." He paused. "I didn't believe it."

"What do you mean?"

"I have trouble explaining it to myself. I know the earth is dead. That's a scientific fact, and I live by facts. But maybe these beings that speak through Kabrina influenced me more than I realized. My intellect tells me it's all over, but my heart has hope."

"For what?"

He shrugged. "For us. For all of humanity."

I nodded. "I have hope, too."

But I didn't tell him what for.

22

In all this time, I had never probed my personal computer file to see how many letters Tem had written me. Perhaps I was afraid he had tired of writing as the years went by, that the frequency of the letters had dwindled, that his devotion had died. If I was realistic, I knew he must have met someone else, and probably gotten married. But what was the point in being a realist when I was still

in love with him? Really, he had never died inside
me.

I had never felt him die.

I was shocked to find that there were only sixty
letters from Tem.

He had written for precisely five years, then had
stopped.

"God," I whispered as I studied the file. "Maybe
he was killed in an accident."

How much I wanted to peek ahead to see what
had been going on in his life just before the letters
stopped. But I had promised him, and I couldn't
break that promise.

*I heard what you whispered to me, about how I
wasn't getting away from you. Paige, I need to tell
you this. I hope a part of you understands . . . You
were right.*

Why had he said that? The only way we could
have met again is if he had boarded the next time-
dilation ship. And that was unlikely because he had
no direct connection to the Space Federation, as I
had. His credentials would not have qualified him
for special consideration. After all, he was just a
frog specialist.

*"What you most wish for, what you most hope
for—that is your greatest illusion. The greatest
barrier that separates you from the Creation."*

I tried not to think about it.

But it was all I could think about.

23

A week later we were all gathered in the garden. We had our alien clone: fully grown, tied down, wired up. She lay on the grass before Kabrina and myself. She was as disgusting looking as her last incarnation. Number One had pulled off a series of brilliant maneuvers to allow us to recapture the pod, taxing the *Traveler*'s hull in the process. We had almost blown ourselves up, he said when we finally had the shuttle back on board.

The alien looked neither happy nor sad to be out of the black container, which made sense to us. As far as human science was concerned, this clone was a blank slate. It may have had a potentially high IQ but its memory banks were empty. It knew nothing of green crystals, we were quite sure, and yet it was supposed to tell us how to build one. Through me, of all people.

Yet the super beings had implied that its cells knew everything.

CHRISTOPHER PIKE

"Am I supposed to mind meld with it or what?" I muttered as we waited for everyone to get seated.

"That sounds kinky," Kabrina said, her eyes open, reading my lips.

I snorted. "For you maybe. You have to remember this is the clone of the monster who killed my father."

"I'm sorry," Kabrina said. "I had forgotten."

"I wish I could do the same," I said softly, feeling a spasm of pain at the memory.

Number One finished setting up the sound system so that the rest of the crew could hear. He sat down beside us. Naturally, every word Kabrina and I said would be recorded. Number One gestured to Kabrina and myself.

"Are you ready?" he asked.

"How do you get ready for something like this?" I asked.

"Relax," Kabrina said. "It's a pleasant experience."

"I just don't want to have to touch it," I said for maybe the tenth time.

We felt a hush in the air. A comforting warmth.

"Let's close our eyes," Kabrina said, closing her own.

I had never sat with my eyes closed in the presence of the super beings. Their power, if anything, seemed magnified. I felt as if I were sliding into a delicious bath of joy.

"We come in love and peace," they said. "We

80

understand many of you wonder what to call us. Where we stand in the Creation, there are no names, no words. We communicate by intention alone. Yet we see great beauty in the spoken word, and for that reason we will give you a name to use to refer to us." A pause. "Alosha."

"To us, that sounds like a feminine name," Number One said. "Are you female?"

"No. We have no sex. But the name vibrates with our essence. Do you like it?"

"Yes, Alosha," Number One said. "It's very beautiful. But are you an individual? Or many? You refer to yourself as we?"

"The concepts have no meaning to us. We are one. We are many. We are Alosha." A pause. "We are here to serve."

"Can you help us obtain the knowledge of how to manufacture the green crystals?" Number One asked.

"Yes. We congratulate you on your technology and daring in constructing and recovering the clone." A pause. "Paige Christian must take the hands of the clone in her hands."

My eyes popped open. "No way."

Number One smiled faintly and patted me on the back. "Pretend you're stealing its knowledge in revenge for what it stole from you."

His words struck me hard. I felt my eyes dampen. "I still want revenge." I spoke to Kabrina, to Alosha. "Will my desire obstruct the process?"

"No. Close your eyes and take the Shamere's hands. You will find it an interesting experience, Paige Christian."

I did as I was told. The clone's skin was wrinkled, slimy—I had to force myself not to let go. But I could feel Alosha's peace stealing over me once more. Taking a few deep breaths, I began to relax more. When they spoke next, through Kabrina, it was as if from far away.

"That which we hate, we feel in ourselves," Alosha said. "That which we fear, we see in others. But hate and fear both arise in the heart, as does love. Hate can conquer fear, but only love can conquer hate. You hate the Shamere in order to protect you from your fear of them. But there is a greater protection." A pause. "See them as not separate from yourself. See them as family. It is easy to love one's family."

"I can't," I whispered, although something was happening that I couldn't explain. It was as if a huge knot were loosening in the region of my heart. For a moment the ghastly images of my father's ruptured body flashed through my mind, only to be replaced by a gentle red glow. I didn't know what I was seeing, only that I prayed it never left me. As the red light increased in brilliance, I felt touched by the hand of God.

"You can. Go back, Paige Christian," Alosha said. "In time and space. A ship floats in the void. It is not this ship nor is it the alien vessel that attacked you. It is another ship, and aboard it you are standing staring at the stars. You know these constellations, their relationship to the evolutionary plan, and you know what you have to do. The task is not easy but you are equal to it. You have gone through a great deal to arrive at this time and place. You have accumulated tremendous knowledge. You understand the Shamere as no one else can. Their wealth of technology—it belongs to you. But you are happy to share it because of your love for the Creation, and all the creatures in it: the Shamere as well as humanity. They are really not so different from you when you remember all that you have learned. The stars help you remember. That is why you love them so much." A pause. "You have only to think of how the crystals are manufactured, and the knowledge is there." A pause. "You remember, Paige Christian?"

The words were not mere suggestions. A great power suddenly took hold of me. A supernova of intuition that blasted me into a realm of insight beyond human fantasy.

I was flying through empty space. I spoke from the other side of the galaxy.

"I remember," I whispered. And I did.

Number One asked me the details and I gave them to him.

24

We now possessed a power greater than that which drove the stars. Our carefully constructed crystals were as strong as the Shamere's originals. Once again our graviton drive blazed with a glory that both exhilarated us and scared us to death. A wave of crushing density spread out around our vessel, and at last the *Traveler* began to apply the brakes. Our mad spin around the solar system began to slow.

We became aware of exactly where the other starship was.

We altered our orbit to rendezvous.

It was now only a few hours away.

Alosha wanted to speak.

I read Tem's next letter before attending the session. His eighth.

Paige,
    As I write this letter, I know everything has changed for you. The girl I met beside the lake

is gone. A mature woman stands in her place, and she is about to confront a great mystery. Don't ask me how I know this, I just do. It is as if your guardian angel stands at my shoulder and whispers ancient secrets in my ear. Unfortunately, she does not say what advice to give you. I doubt there is any that can prepare you for what you are about to go through. I just wish I could be with you, in your future, and hold you and tell you it will be all right.

I know, I'm dead now—how can I give you hope? And I know hope is not the answer. Maybe love is. I can give you that, even now, ever so late. I can love you and believe that my love will find you wherever you are, and give you strength. From the beginning, I knew you were stronger than I am. I think that's why you were chosen to go. Please don't regret your choice.

Love,
Tem

I didn't understand his letter.
Not at all. But it scared me.

25

Kabrina sat with her eyes closed, her deaf ears tuned to our inquiries. Outside, the earth ship grew closer. Why couldn't Alosha wait until after docking to give us our next lesson? I decided there must be something we needed to know to prepare us for the momentous occasion.

"What are the seven steps along the path?" Number One asked.

"We will begin," Alosha said, and then took a long pause. "The first step toward the truth of the Creation is discrimination. Discrimination between what? The real and the unreal. That is the key element. No progress is realized until it is achieved. Yet, when you left earth, as a people, perhaps one in a million had achieved discrimination. That is why the destruction of earth occurred. It had to occur, for your own sakes."

There was a buzz in the garden. Alosha wasn't winning any friends this afternoon. She/he/we/it was just confusing us. Number One spoke for all of us with his next question.

"Could you please clarify?" he said.

"We understand your difficulty in accepting this concept. Part of this is because of your misunderstanding of the purpose of human life, and your ideas of what is real." A pause. "Time is a ruler set down by the Creation to measure progress. Time allows you to have linear experiences. If there was no time, nothing could be learned. A test must be timed—if it is not, the test results are invalid. You practice this in your classrooms, in your highest as well as your lowest systems of education. In the same way, the Creation is one huge classroom. You enter it to learn—to learn you are the Creation. But you cannot take all your lessons at once, so the Creation divides them up for you. At least you think they are divided. In reality you are handed the whole textbook at once. But the pages, the many lives you live, are turned one at a time." A pause. "Do you understand?"

Number One frowned. "Are you talking about reincarnation? Are you saying humanity evolves through many lives?"

"Yes and no. There cannot be many lives when there is no time. For us time does not exist. For you it does exist. What is true for us is not necessarily true for you. You may believe in reincarnation, but we see all your lives as occurring at once." A pause. "We must expand on this."

"Please continue," Number One said.

"Let us take the life of a soul entering time. He dives into the Creation and at first there is much to experience: the pleasures of the five senses; the expansion of the intellect; the adventures of new lands—all these things the Creation gives to the soul. And so many lives go by in this way. He gets married and has children. He becomes a brilliant scientist or a foolish bum. He fights in wars and kills many, and then he in turn is killed as he strives to create peace. He becomes a priest and he becomes a prostitute, a saint and then a sinner, a female and a male. The soul goes around and around and he tries just about everything.

"But then one day he gets tired of it all and begins to look for something else. This craving for something else grows particularly strong after many lifetimes of tragedy. You see tragedy as something to avoid at all costs. But we see it as a strong stimulus to develop discrimination.

"Imagine you are back in the nineteenth century. You are a pioneer settling the wild West. The unexplored country is beautiful but untamed. You have your wife and children with you. You build a fine cabin and you start to farm the surrounding land. But then a gang of bandits storm in one night and murder your wife and children. They burn down your cabin and destroy your land and crops. In one night you have lost all you have worked to build. Your heart is broken. You cradle your dead wife and children in your arms and you swear at

God for letting such a thing happen. All hope dies inside. Everything seems worthless.

"But in that state a change takes place deep inside you. You see that you can no longer trust in the things of the world. They are always changing, always dying—there is no stability there. You begin to search elsewhere for something that does not change. We said discrimination was knowing the real from the unreal. We will tell you what the real is—it is that which does not change. Many lives make you crave it—the eternal. It is only after many difficult trials that one seeks the path to the Creation."

Number One interrupted. "We have religions. People put their faith in those."

"Religion is man-made. It is not eternal. It is not real. At first, it may relieve a soul from the horrors of the world, but that relief does not last. It brings no true contentment. One can join every religion there is, yet the longing for the real does not vanish. It does not matter if you try to convince yourself that it has left. It continues to grow over many lives. Where is the real? Where is the eternal? The soul becomes obsessed to find it. Then the man rejects all religions, all philosophies, all belief systems. He doesn't want to believe in anything. He has no opinions. He just craves what has always been there from the beginning—himself. His inner self. Then, finally, he can be said to be a seeker of the Creation."

There was a long pause. It seemed as if no one breathed. Number One finally stirred. "We are still confused," he said. "You said the earth had to be destroyed for our benefit. Why? Was it to give us all a sense of the impermanence of things?"

"Precisely. Each of you was deeply affected by the earth's destruction. Almost overnight you developed discrimination, on a scale that could not have been achieved had another million years elapsed. You saw with your own eyes that nothing was permanent. As a race you made a huge leap on the path."

"But that makes no sense," Number One said. "As a race we were wiped out."

"Many survived out amongst the stars. And those many multiplied, and began to look deep inside themselves. No longer did they put their faith in man-made instruments or beliefs. Finally, they desired the real—that which does not change."

"What is the second step on the path?" Number One asked.

"Kindness. A prophet named Jesus taught the first two steps of the path to the Creation, but only the first two. His gospel was simple: the kingdom of God is inside you, and you should love your neighbor. Love is the same as kindness. Jesus did not say God is up in heaven somewhere. He possessed profound discrimination, but few of his followers did. He spoke of the need to look inside for the real, and he spoke of the need to express the real through acts of kindness. The more love a man or woman has, the easier it is to take the third step on the path."

"What is the third step?" Number One asked.

"You are curious?"

"Yes. We're all curious."

There was a long pause.

"We want you to consider what has been said before we continue. We want you to meet your friends on the other ship, and then you will naturally desire to return to earth. You have a few experiences left before you can move on. A couple of them will surprise you." A long pause. "We leave you in love and peace."

Alosha was gone. My fear was not.

I knew in my heart I had no discrimination.

I still wanted Tem, fragile human love. It was all I wanted.

I prayed he was alive on the other ship.

26

The earth vessel floated before us and already there was a mystery. Half the ship was missing. There were living quarters but no propulsion system. Earth had sent it into time dilation orbit, but who had decided it should never decelerate? Unlit except by the distant red sun, it was a dark box filled with either black despair or miraculous joy. I kept telling myself I had never felt him die, that I should have if he had died. But I knew the odds of his being aboard the ship were a million to one.

Number One let me accompany him over in the shuttle.

He had heard about Tem from Kabrina. He knew about my hopes.

He gestured to the swelling bulk. Even missing her engines, the ship was twice the size of the *Traveler*. How many human Popsicles did it hold? Five thousand? Despite Alosha's words, I had to wonder how any of them could have survived over the many millennia. Number One spoke my fears aloud.

"This ship was placed in a high dilation orbit," he said. "Still millions of years have elapsed for it."

"But things do not age in space," I said.

"People are not things. Even with an advanced hibernation system, I will be surprised if any of them survived."

"Alosha says they are alive," I replied.

Number One was thoughtful. "I wonder if I offended Alosha with my questions. Why were the seven steps left incomplete, when they obviously meant to give them out earlier?"

I shook my head. "It was nothing you said. It was our reaction to the information. I love Alosha, and I did not want to accept it. Discrimination is still a goal. The unreal still seems so real to me. I kept thinking of that man who lost his family on the western frontier. I don't think I could bear that."

"You have borne a great deal in the last few months."

He was hinting that I might be on the verge of another trauma. "I have no hope," I said as I stared at the closing vessel. I could now read a name on the side—the *Pandora*. A chill shook me from head to toe. I was familiar with the Pandora myth, how many vices were unleashed on humankind. Why had they called the ship that?

Number One nodded. "I hope you mean that."

27

Inside was a mass graveyard. There was no artificial gravity. There was no air; it had been purposely ventilated to prevent corrosion, so we assumed. We wore space suits. The hibernaculums floated in the inky cavern, ghosts haunting a ship that could never sink. They were chained down, of course, but there was so many of them, piled one on top of the other. Our exploratory party estimated there were at least twenty thousand.

We did a quick scan of their instrumentation.

It was still functioning. We activated their computers.

There was a list of passengers.

Tem was number 13,567.

28

I floated by Tem's hibernaculum. I was out of my suit. Air had been restored to the *Pandora.* I stared into Tem's face plate. There was a fine layer of frost over the glass, but I could see him: his long dark braided hair; his powerful face; even his smile. He had fallen asleep grinning, perhaps thinking of the joke he had played on me by not dying. My tears, as they dripped onto the face plate, turned to ice. That was OK; I brushed them with my lips and they melted. I was kissing him. The revival process had just begun, but I wasn't worried. Already we had thawed out a thousand friends and every one of them was in excellent health.

It was just a matter of time before Tem was in my arms again.

My joy then was a gift from God.

Number One and Kabrina came by to check on the progress of 13,567. Kabrina could not stop smiling, seeing how happy I was. Right then, more than ever before, I felt gratitude for Alosha, for making this miracle possible. So the earth was dead, I thought. With love, we could make it bloom again. With love, we could light up the whole galaxy.

Number One checked the monitor on Tem's hibernaculum.

His cheek twitched. He stared at me.

I stared back. "What's the matter?" I asked.

"There's something wrong," he said.

I froze. "There can't be anything wrong," I whispered.

Kabrina moved up beside her father. "Is it serious?" she asked.

Number One worked the controls on the life-support monitor. "We're not getting a brain-wave reading. And we should have a heartbeat by now."

"He could be taking longer than the others," Kabrina said.

"No." Number One removed his fingers from the monitor controls. He turned his head to the side and stared at nothing. How much he looked like my father right then, when my father had told me there was no going back home. Such an idea—to ever return to a world of water and life—suddenly seemed ridiculous. He didn't have to tell me. Billions of years had gone by. I had waited through each second of them for this moment. I had begged to stand in this moment beside the guy I loved. But this moment was cursed.

"He's dead." I paused as my voice cracked. "Is he?"

Number One sighed. "He died a long time ago, Paige."

29

Another week went by. We had recovered a total of 22,678 people from the *Pandora*. Besides Tem, only one other had failed to revive, a woman named Heila Derby. She had been only twenty-five years old, about the same age as Tem. Both of them, it seemed, had died shortly after entering their hibernaculums. Our engineers were still checking the situation out, but they could find no reason for the two deaths.

We floated toward the earth. Finally we were back in normal time. The sun had already passed through its red giant phase. Now it was only ten times bigger than when we had left earth; its surface was no longer brushing the orbit of Venus. But its light was feeble; it gave off only a hundredth the warmth it used to. Earth was not only alone it was cold, so very cold. Just like the rest of the universe.

Over nine billion years had passed since we left home.

I stood on the observation deck and stared at the sun and the earth. Our various shuttles would be departing within an hour to land and explore the dust and rocks that now covered the earth from pole to pole. What we were looking for, I couldn't imagine.

The *Pandora* was not just a repository of hibernaculums. We had towed it back home with us because it possessed large quantities of supplies, enough, almost, to supply a budding civilization. But I thought we should go elsewhere, and leave the earth to rest. I had told Number One my opinion, but like the majority of others, he hated to leave so soon, after we had struggled so long to return.

I understood many things. Yet I still did not comprehend why it was so painful to learn such simple lessons. I wondered if Alosha had halted the seven steps because of me. My agony was tearing me apart and still I was afraid to let it go. He was dead; I needed to let his memory go, too. That was the first step for me, before discrimination.

Yet my love was the ghost of a young girl's dream. It walked alone in the abyss, stubbornly, where only illusions prospered on tears and regrets. My love had a life of its own; it was perverted but nevertheless still vital. For that reason, I wanted to return to deep space. Honestly, I would have preferred it if we had traveled forever and never stopped at another star system. To fall into endless blackness, that was my new fantasy.

The young girl with the ancient dream wept. I could hear her; I even saw her tears on the glass of the observation deck. It made me feel old. I didn't want to know her name. I couldn't forget Tem but I needed to forget her.

I had asked Number One for a shuttle of my own.

To return Tem to earth, and bury him where we had met.

Within the hour, I would lay him in his grave.

"Never is a long time," I whispered as I recalled what he had told me the day we said goodbye. "Even for us."

30

Using our incredible technology, I was able to find the location of Rainbow Park. I even found the precise spot beside the lake where we had met. I set the shuttle down in what would have been the center of the lake. After climbing out, I was forced to wear a respirator and breathe bottled air. The air was too thin to breathe.

How sad it all was. The sun was a swollen pumpkin on the horizon. It looked sick—an inflated plastic toy left out for a Halloween where only real monsters came knocking. Monsters who ended up killing those who offered them candy. I stared at the sun and couldn't believe it was the same one that had shone over my shoulder as I skipped down the stairs of the library that fateful afternoon, nine billion years ago. Its sober red light was the color of a twilight that had for too long felt the chill of the coming night. The only trouble with this approaching night was that it would never end.

I wondered then what it would be like to see the Creation end.

I walked around the area. The red dust stirred beneath my feet. I tasted the salt of a lost sea, and wondered if the ocean had eventually covered the area. The plain on which I stood was not entirely flat. In the distance I could see pillars of stone, their edges well worn. The wind was feeble but it had been blowing for eons. I knew if I were to touch the pillars, they would crumble.

I found the spot where I had met Tem. Sitting down in the dust, I closed my eyes and clutched his lock of hair to my heart. Try as I might, I could not visualize the park: the grass, the water, or the trees. But I could imagine his smile. He was still smiling as he lay in the shuttle, a few feet away.

I stood up and fetched his body, which was no longer frozen.

I had only a shovel. I wanted to feel the dust as I dug.

I laid him beside the hole as I shoveled away dirt.

The work was hard and I had to rest frequently. My mask filled with foggy sweat. I briefly removed it and tried to breathe what was left of the earth's atmosphere. But I ended up coughing. Still, I kept trying to get something out of the air. I felt compelled. This world was my mother. I felt I must show her that I still needed her to live.

I was in the middle of my third coughing fit when I felt the presence.

I stopped digging and looked around.

"Hello?" I said. "If you're there, I could really use your wonderful words. I'm not feeling that good. The only trouble is, Kabrina's not here. And I don't think I'm high enough to pick up the higher telepathy."

Nobody spoke.

But I felt a compulsion to sit down and close my eyes.

I went with it. I had nowhere else to go.

I waited. Time passed. The thin wind rustled.

No words of wisdom came to me.

Then I heard a sound. Someone sitting up.

Someone near. I opened my eyes.

"Hello," he said.

Oh God.

31

He was not God but was closer to God than he was to the Tem I had once known. Just a glance at his eyes and I knew I was not sitting beside a human being. There was a light inside him that shone from eternity. He was the *real* thing—no discrimination was needed to see that.

But maybe I was wrong.

"Alosha," I whispered through my mask.

He smiled slightly as he stretched his arms and legs. Slowly he looked around, at the sea of dust, the fading sun. The thin air didn't seem to bother him.

"You may call me Tem if you wish." He spoke with Tem's vocal cords, but there was an authority in his tone that no human could match. Yet there was kindness there as well, a soothing whisper that a concerned parent might speak with to a distraught child.

"I can't," I whispered.

His eyes came to rest on me and he patted the ground beside him. "Sit here, close. These eyes want to see you."

I did as I was told. I moved close enough to touch him.

"You can touch me," he said. "I don't mind."

I shook my head slightly. "But you're not him. You're Alosha. I feel that."

He nodded. "But who is Alosha? Who to you?"

"Why? Why speak to us?"

"We are bound to you with a thread of love."

"Is Alosha what Tem evolved into over nine billion years?" I asked.

"Yes. You understand, Paige Christian. I am here. I said I would see you again and I have. It was a promise, and now I have kept that promise."

I choked. "Oh Jesus."

His smile widened. "He made promises that he also kept, when he returned." He paused, and an inexplicable note of sorrow entered his voice. "But that was a long time ago."

"Why did you come back?" I asked.

His easy tone returned. "I just told you. But I understand, you seek a deeper reason. I don't know if I can give you one." He paused. "Aren't you happy to see me?"

Tears came, soft and silently. "Yes. I can't tell you how happy I am. But I'm also grieved. You're not like me. You're a million times what I am. I'm afraid of you now."

He did not try to argue the point. "The Creation has gone forward while you have stood still."

I remembered the words. "I am a seed that never saw the harvest." A wave of sorrow swept over me. "I am a lost soul."

"No. You are not lost. You have merely lost your way. That is not the same as being lost. But that also was destined. You, Paige Christian, and you alone are supposed to live in the same physical body through a span of two Creations. Take heart —it is a unique privilege."

I gasped. "What are you talking about?"

"You have to return to your ship. You have to take it when the others leave it. You have to sail out beyond the farthest star, at a speed so close to that of light that all of what is left of time passes in the twinkle of a star. In that void, you will see the Creation fall back in on itself. The dead stars, the burnt-out galaxies—they will all begin to rush toward a single point. And when they reach it, there will be an explosion of light and energy, and a new Creation will begin. Then you will turn your ship around and sail back to that time and place just before you left the earth. There you will find a new earth, identical to the one you left long ago." He paused. "There you will find another humanity."

I couldn't take it all in. "That's impossible."

"It is the way it is and the way it will be."

"The Creation repeats itself? Exactly?"

"Yes and no. These things cannot be explained

with words. I am only permitted to tell you so much." He paused and reached out to take my hand. His touch was warm. "You have to go forward. You have to become what I am. Only then can you be with me. With all of us, for we are all one."

I heard Tem right then. "But I'm with you now."

"Only for these few minutes."

"But why can't I just go with you now? Why can't you raise me up to your level? I hate it down here in the dirt. All this Creation gives me is pain and then more pain."

"You know the reason for that."

"But I can't learn this discrimination! It's too hard. I want what I can touch and feel and hold close to my heart. I don't know anything else except that."

"That is precisely what you must find." He paused. "We will see to your friends aboard the *Traveler*. They have the knowledge and the tools to survive here. They want to be here. But this place holds nothing for you. This Creation is dead to you, and you know that. But in the next one you will complete the cycle of life. Then it will be finished for you, and you will rest in eternity."

Now my tears gushed out, and I gripped his hand tightly.

"Don't leave me," I pleaded. "I can't stand to see you for this short time and then have you go."

He brushed a tear from my face beside my mask. "I can't stay, Paige Christian. I'm sorry."

I spoke quickly, in case he suddenly faded. "Tell me what it's like where you are now? What is it like to be one with the Creation?"

His gaze was focused far away. "It is a wonder. Everything is always new. My ocean washes upon many mysterious shores. There is always adventure and excitement, yet everything has already been revealed. It is a paradox. The secret of every riddle has been solved. There is nothing but light and joy—it permeates all facets of existence. But above all, there is simplicity." He paused. "You think of me as a god, but I am the simplest of men."

I forced a smile. "Do you still like frogs?"

"Of course." He smiled and released my hand. He stood and stared out at the vast dust plain that had once been the green park where we wandered at will. I climbed to my feet as he raised his arms and let the red sun shine over his limbs. Soon the sun would set, as it had set when I last said goodbye. He spoke seriously. "You know what you have to do."

I shook my head. "It sounds impossible."

"Not for you." He brushed my hair with his fingertips, stared at my face. Gently, he reached up and removed my mask. His lips, as they touched my lips, were sweet. I didn't need to breathe, as long as they were near me. A greater power than breathing kept me alive. But then he pulled back and smiled again, his old Tem smile, the mischievous one. "Are you the first page or the last?" he asked.

"I guess the answer is that I'm both."

"Even then, I knew that about you." He briefly touched my heart, then he turned away and gazed at the setting sun. The red glow on his skin was grim, but the light on his face was joyful. "Time is nothing to us, Paige."

"This moment is forever," I whispered, replacing my mask.

He sighed faintly, but there was no regret in it. "You remembered; I knew you would." He stepped down the slope away from me. "Goodbye," he said.

"Goodbye," I said.

He walked into the sun. The dust stirred, the sun set.

It grew dark and cold. He was gone.

32

He said I had a unique destiny. Back aboard the *Traveler*, it felt like a curse. I couldn't share in the excitement of the others as they talked of how they would rebuild the earth. Because I was planning to stab them in the backs. To steal one of their ships.

The problems to overcome were daunting. First, one person could not operate the *Traveler*. It was too big a ship. True, I could fire up the engines and take it out of earth orbit. That required nothing but a few pushed buttons. But the engines needed regular attention—I couldn't maintain them alone. Yet I knew I would have to worry about that later. If it was my destiny to succeed, and see the next Creation, then I would overcome.

My other main problem was how I was going to get everyone off the ship. The *Traveler* could be in earth orbit the next hundred years and there wouldn't be a day when it was totally unoccupied. Obviously I was going to have to force everyone off.

The only way I could figure to do that would be to set the ship to explode, or rather, to set it so that it *appeared* it would explode with no chance of stopping the explosion. Even then Number One might stay. He was now the captain and would probably feel it was his duty to go down with his ship. Well, he couldn't do that. I couldn't have the guilt of his death haunting me in the next Creation.

I had to arrange for my surprise when Number One was away.

And incredibly I knew exactly how to do it. Since mind linking with the Shamere clone, I had begun to experience extraordinary insights into physics, engineering, and genetics. As I walked the long halls of the *Traveler,* I often thought of how I could make the ship ten times more efficient. The alterations seemed obvious to me, and I knew the reason. While attached to the Shamere, the alien's advanced knowledge had impressed itself on my cells. I was probably the smartest human left alive in the galaxy, but it wasn't something I bragged about. To simulate a graviton drive overload, I would need a green crystal and a few minutes alone in the engine room.

I got my chance one month after we had entered earth orbit.

Number One was planet side, overseeing the completion of a ten-mile-wide pressurized dome where the majority of our people would be transferred in a couple of days. I was in the garden with Kabrina, where so many extraordinary things had happened recently. I had an eye on the engine room monitor. I knew the place was to be closed down briefly for a robotic cleaning, which employed high levels of radiation.

Kabrina was trying to console me about Tem.

"I didn't tell you," I interrupted. "I spoke to him."

She stopped and stared at me. "I didn't catch what you said," she said. "Could you please repeat?"

I signed out the words. Kabrina just shook her head.

"Paige. It's not possible."

I shook my head. "You know, I think we underestimated those we left behind. We thought in two hundred years they would develop all kinds of wonderful inventions. But I think they did more than make new toys." I paused. "I wonder where the other half of the *Pandora* went."

"To another star system. You heard what their commander said."

"Yeah. But he didn't look like he was telling the whole story." I was thoughtful. "Maybe he didn't know it."

Kabrina was confused. "What has this got to with Tem?"

"He came back to see me. He fulfilled his promise to me. He didn't even ask for all the letters I didn't send him." I patted Kabrina's arm. "It doesn't matter. That was another life. I have to let it go. I have . . . things to do." Leaning over, I kissed

111

her cheek and whispered in her ear, so she couldn't possibly hear me. "I love you, Kabrina. But now I have to say goodbye. I'm never going to see you again, and that is much too long a time to be separated from you. Believe me, I know."

I drew back. Maybe she heard more than I thought.

There were tears on her face. Maybe they had washed from mine.

"What is happening, Paige?" she asked.

"History," I said, turning away, where she could no longer read my lips. "The end of history."

33

The doors to the engine room were sealed shut. The cleansing of the graviton engine with the heavy cosmic radiation hadn't started yet, but I had to manipulate the lock to get inside anyway. I automatically unlocked it—how to do it came to me in vivid waves of pictures and symbols I did not consciously recognize. It seemed there was nothing about our technology that the Shamere hadn't known.

That fact continued to puzzle me.

I locked myself in the engine room and shorted out all the viewing monitors. Around me, various robots were preparing to discharge the radiation directly into the engines. Using a nearby monitor, I tapped into the ship's central computer and was able to disable the robots as well. I knew right about now the officers on the bridge would be having anxiety attacks. And I was just getting started.

After putting on a protective suit, I crossed through the barrier toward our plasma stream. I intended to use a green crystal to simulate a massive meltdown of the graviton core. I had several crystals in my pocket. Alone, I had manufactured them in our lab.

I opened up the core and placed the crystal inside.

The plasma stream ate it up.

Once again, the noise and light was both deafening and blinding. I retreated to the elevator and placed the transparent barrier between myself and the engines. Yet it was possible I had already absorbed a lethal dose of radiation. At the moment I didn't care. I was not in free-will mode. I felt everything I was doing had been set up by the Creation.

A red alert sounded. I heard people banging on the door. I didn't let them in, but I did reconnect communications to the bridge. Someone spoke from a simple audio speaker. I recognized Officer Bella—a tough old cookie who had worshiped the ground my father walked on. She was Number One's right hand person.

"Who's in engineering?" she demanded.

"Just me," I said.

There was an incredulous pause. "Paige? What are you doing?"

"I have set the graviton drive to explode. If you consult the core readings, you will see that you have less than ten minutes to abandon ship."

There was another long pause. Then seething outrage.

"Why have you done this?" Bella demanded. "The ship is ruined!"

"You better get off now. By the way, if you try to break into engineering, I will immediately explode the core. I have a few extra green crystals on me. You remember I was the one who came up with the formula for making them."

"But why are you doing this?" Bella screamed again.

"I don't know. It must be that time of month."

I cut the line. There was no sense trying to explain.

34

Ten minutes later the ship was empty. I checked all
the monitors, all the sensors. I was the only living
creature on board. Effortlessly, using physical prin-
ciples that had yet to be invented, I reversed the
meltdown, bleeding the excess energy off into a
massive gravity wave displacement. The *Traveler*
blasted out of orbit. I imagined, down on earth,
they could see me leaving. I wonder what they all
thought, when the ship did not explode. Especially,
I wondered what Kabrina thought of me. But I
knew they would be all right with the *Pandora* and
the almost completed dome.

I was alone as no human being had ever been
alone. Sailing out beyond the orbit of Pluto, past
the cometary cloud, I had no idea which direction
to go. Where was the center of the Creation? How
did I turn away from it without knowing? This time
the Shamere knowledge did not come to my rescue.

The aliens had not solved every mystery of the physical universe.

Using the crystals, I boosted my speed dramatically. This time there was no six-month period of acceleration. The sun was a vanishing red star a week after I left. Again the clock spun crazily—I was in extreme time dilation, which meant Kabrina and the others were long dead.

It was taking me millions of years to get to where I was going, but for me, they passed in a daydream of friends and foes while I stared out the wide window on the observation deck. Below me, I saw the almost extinguished spiral body of the Milky Way fall away. How sorry I felt for it then, that such a magnificent galaxy could be humbled by time. The few stars that still shone were like tiny lights placed inside a massive corpse. The center of the galaxy, the heart, was black as coal.

My skills were endless. Maybe I was an alien. I refashioned the mindless robotic servants into master maintenance engineers. They worked the graviton drive twenty-four hours a day, always tinkering, constantly refining the plasma stream. I didn't have to do anything; they did it all. They even said hello to me and inquired about my well being as I walked by. I had taught them to speak in addition to everything else.

Intergalactic space was my next stop, and still I continued to press the last finite point off my velocity and the speed of light. Time continued to dilate, and the millions of years of elapsed time turned again into billions. I began to have trouble finding galaxies in the black sky. The second law of athermodynamics was being played out. Entropy always increased. The universe was running down.

Then I began to notice strange phenomena. In the far distance, I saw a faint violet glow, and numerous gaseous ghosts flying toward it. This glow and the ghosts—at first I didn't understand what they were. I was tempted to turn my ship in that direction. Despite my earlier vow, the endless black was beginning to oppress me. I wanted to turn toward the light, perhaps even feel its warmth. But then the truth of the matter occurred to me.

The ghosts were the remains of the dead galaxies.

The violet glow was the mother of all black holes.

It was drawing what was left of the universe back into itself. It would have got me if I hadn't been moving so fast.

I had to get some distance from it and quick. Turning the *Traveler* away from the glow, I poured more green crystals into the plasma stream. Now the amount of elapsed time lost all meaning. Yet the violet glow did not grow in intensity, as I expected. I did not know if that was because most of the universe had already been absorbed or because I was too far from it to see clearly what was happening. I only knew that I was heading into the final nothingness.

I sang to myself. The words died in the air around me, even when I stood in the garden. Gathering my robotic helpers, I lectured them about what it meant to be human, and they mechanically applauded every time I paused. Lying alone on my bed in my room, I imagined Tem resting beside me. But the bed always felt so empty.

One day I went to the observation deck and noticed the violet glow was gone. Consulting the ship's main telescope, I was unable to detect even a trace of it. In every direction, there was only the void. And I wondered why God was always associated with light. The true supreme being who swallowed the Creation at the finish of time was as black as a bottomless well. I even wondered if time itself could be called God. Certainly, in the end, it had defeated everything else.

Except perhaps me.

"It's over," I said. To no one in particular.

35

The feeling then was like a prolonged hush. A breath inhaled but never exhaled. I walked the empty halls of the *Traveler* and tried not to think about how long they would remain silent. For in reality, it was the absolute silence of everything that had begun to disturb me even more than the endless black and the bitter cold. I could hear my heart beat and it seemed to me a sin, that anything should move in this soundless chasm. Far away, in another dimension perhaps, I tried to convince myself that a major masterpiece was on the verge of taking birth. A new Creation to sing and dance and play in.

But I could not feel the approaching birth.

Any more than I had felt Tem's death.

Only death pangs. My heart seemed to echo in my chest.

I wondered if the rest of my life would go by like this.

It was a thought born of despair.

36

There was another special time, during that week I had known Tem. We sat on a high hill overlooking Rainbow Park. It was almost morning; the sun was just coloring the east. We sat facing each other with our eyes closed. We didn't know what we were doing, maybe meditating, maybe being silly. Tem had just wanted to try the experiment. But he had given me no idea what the results would be, and because it was so early and we had been up so late the night before, I fell asleep. My head just fell forward on my chest as I sat there.

I dreamed I was in a crystal cave. Everywhere, the walls were covered with glowing jewels: amethysts, sapphires, emeralds, rubies—they fanned a haunting rainbow over my hands and face. Staring at the gems, I was filled with the inexpressible certainty that I was seeing a great secret. Something no mortal was supposed to see.

In the dream, I came to a dark pond, whose

surface shone faintly with the glow of the jewels. I sat down to rest, for I was tired, and at first I thought I was alone. But then I realized there was someone sitting across the pond from me. His eyes were closed and he seemed to be deep in mystical communion. I didn't want to bother him, but an unexpected loneliness touched me then.

"Tem?" I whispered.

He opened his eyes and they glowed with a strange violet light.

"Paige," he said. But it was not the dream person.

It was the real Tem, shaking me awake. He had dozed as well.

He'd had the exact same dream.

Except in his, my eyes were the ones that shone with light.

37

I thought of writing Tem a letter. It was my turn.
But there was nothing new to tell him.

38

Let there be light. It started without warning.
I was eating a breakfast of orange juice, coffee,
toast, and eggs when the Creation began. Fortu-
nately I was stuffing my face on the observation
deck. I was able to see the very beginning. Far in the

distance there was a peculiar soundless flash, like the explosion of an underwater creature's fireworks. A wave of longing swept over me suddenly, for feelings, perhaps, that would not exist in the next Creation. Then I was forced to close my eyes because the light became blinding.

A tidal wave struck the side of my ship.

The *Traveler* hull groaned.

Swept away. Never before had I felt such a rush. I was riding the cosmic wave of existence, and now my heart pounded in my chest with joy. As the glare of the primeval light subsided, I opened my eyes and toasted the new beginning with my glass of orange juice.

"May you live long and be happy," I said. "And hopefully be less a pain in the ass than the last Creation."

39

The ship computer had a record of the *Traveler*'s course, through time and space. Calculating when we had first left earth, and when I had left it the second time, and adding in the actual age of the universe—which I could now list accurately—the computer figured out which way to turn my ship to bring it back to earth in the early twenty-third century. Of course, I had to radically adjust my speed downward.

All around me galaxies were forming and stars were being born.

The sight filled me with awe and gratitude.

All the agony I had gone through . . .

Right then it all seemed worthwhile.

I felt like a mother, I really did.

I thought of the stories I could tell my children.

40

The solar system shone before me. Familiar constellations stood behind me. I was coming in at normal speed and time, but I couldn't come all the way in on a vessel as big as the *Traveler*. I would be spotted, and that wouldn't do. Starting a chain reaction in the plasma stream—this one irreversible—I hurried to the shuttle and left my home for only God knew how many years. As I jettisoned from the belly of the mighty starship, a tear rolled over my cheek. Always, it seemed, I was losing my home. Having to trade it in for another I didn't know and didn't understand.

The *Traveler* exploded even as I whispered goodbye.

Yet the earth looked the same, as I swept toward the heart of the solar system. The sight was reassuring, although my immediate goal was not earth but Mars. I knew it would be easier to land on the fourth planet unobserved, and start a new life, with identification papers I had forged between the Creations, and a face I had altered slightly after the second Big Bang.

My new name was Alpha Book.

I enjoyed the irony. The first page of the story.

But I couldn't take credit for the name. Or could I?

41

It took me three months to make it to new earth. The time I used wisely. I was thinking more about what had happened last time around: the unprovoked attack of the Shamere, the hypnotic gaze of the evil commander, the friendly alien, the disemboweled *Pandora,* the lifeless body of Tem, the kind words of the illumined soul on the dusty plain. There was a pattern here—I was finally beginning to recognize it. I understood what Alosha had meant by the word *destiny*—all the ramifications. I used every spare minute studying genetics. The Shamere knowledge haunted my psyche.

I knew my future but I hated it.

Yes, I understood destiny, and I was sick of it.

One sunny afternoon, I stood on the steps of a library across from a park. Checking my watch, I adjusted my cheap blond wig and dark sunglasses. I had added a fraction of an inch to my nose, altered my cheekbones a tad. But I knew the main changes in me were the invisible scars of all I had gone through. I knew I wouldn't be recognized. Not in a million years.

A pretty redheaded girl came out of the library and skipped down the stairs.

How happy she looked! It broke my heart, honestly.

I had a high-powered laser pistol in my coat pocket. I was in one of those moods again, I suppose. I was sick of the Creation telling me how it was going to be. I stared at her as if I knew her. My gaze stopped her in her tracks. I stepped toward her, feeling the weight of the weapon against my skin, and offered my hand.

"You look like you don't remember me, Paige," I said softly. "I met you a couple years ago. We were introduced at a party for a mutual friend. My name's Alpha Book."

She shook my hand. She acted polite but cautious. "I'm sorry. I know your face, but that's all." She paused. "Who was the friend?"

I forced a smile. My eyes strayed to the nearby park.

"I don't remember," I said. "Isn't that funny?

But I remember you." I pointed to the trees. "I was just there. It's lovely today. You should go. I was sitting by the lake beside the fountain." I lowered my head and knew sorrow touched my features, because I couldn't get over how sweet she was, and how I was going to shoot her in the face in just a few seconds and kill her. I mumbled, "It was very lovely."

This Paige was sweet. "I've never heard the name Alpha before."

Coming to a hard decision, I raised my head. "It suits me, Paige." Then I reached inside my coat, took the handle of the laser, and felt the trigger beneath my sweaty finger. This was my Creation, I thought bitterly. I had earned it. The chance to have a normal life. The chance to love the only guy I could love. And better it should end for this girl now, before she had to replay all the agony I had gone through. Really—I thought I knew what was real—I would be doing her a favor.

Forgive me, Alosha. But sometimes love is not enough.

Standing before me, she stiffened, almost as if she suspected I meant to do her harm. And it was that glimpse of fear that shattered my resolve. Now her murder could not be totally painless. I could not look at her and not love her. And you could not hurt what you loved, unless you had either perfect discrimination, or else none at all. A warm tear formed in the corner of my right eye, and yet it felt cold as it reached for the flesh of my face. My hand shifted from the laser to my handkerchief.

"I should go," I said, dabbing at the tear. "It was nice to see you again."

She hesitated. "You, too."

Turning, I walked down the steps, feeling her eyes on my back. It was all I could do to make it around the side of the library building. There I collapsed in sobs, trembling so violently that I thought I would pass out. Pulling the laser pistol from my coat, I tossed it into a nearby trash can.

Then I went home, to my new home.

An empty apartment I had rented for Alpha Book.

But I refused to be alone forever.

42

The *Traveler* left earth orbit. I watched on TV. The newscasters explained how long it would be gone and perhaps what the world would be like when it returned. It was hard to maintain a straight face when they spoke about such things.

I didn't go see Tem right away, although I was dying to see him. He was supposed to be grieving over me, and I needed to establish myself as a real person. Actually, I had to start working for the Space Federation so that I could somehow get aboard another starship.

Alpha Book was too weird a name, and besides, I needed to improve my false identification, which was no easy a matter. Everybody on earth was in the computers. What was essential was that I find someone who had just died, and convince the authorities that the death had been recorded as an error, that I was the person. Preferably this person should have no family, and few friends.

Heila Derby gave me the perfect opportunity. She died in an avalanche on Triton, the principal moon of Neptune. She was buried along with her whole exploratory party. Doing research, I found her only surviving relation was a half brother, but this guy just happened to have a prison record, a rare case in the twenty-third century. It took me a month to find him, but from various goods I had stolen from the *Traveler,* I was able to bribe him into helping me convince the authorities I was alive and well. By amazing coincidence, I happened to resemble Heila Derby, sort of.

But was it coincidence?

I remembered her name, of course.

I got a job with the Space Federation, in a minor genetics lab. I did grunt work—Heila Derby did not have a doctorate in genetics. But I knew she would start to show amazing promise quickly. I was there only a month when I got promoted. Bit by bit, I began to reveal pieces of the Shamere's knowledge of genetics. My first boss thought I was an undereducated genius. After four months on the job, I was transferred to a larger lab and placed in a program where I could obtain my genetics doctorate in four years. I knew it wouldn't take me half that time.

It was after six months of being on earth that I approached Tem. I was such a clever rascal—I waited for him by the side of the lake in Rainbow Park while he was diving. As he came out of the water, I was sitting in the exact spot his girlfriend had been sitting, when they first met. He did a double take when he saw me. Although my hair was now dyed black and my nose was more pointed—as the real Heila's hair and nose had been—I still looked a lot like Paige Christian. For example, I had left my green eyes alone. I batted them at Tem as he removed his diving mask. That is until he used the same line he had used on me before.

"You don't look like a fish," he said.

Fair was fair.

"In case you didn't notice, you've already surfaced," I said.

He blinked, puzzled. I had to be careful not to go too far with the old quotes. I couldn't exactly tell him who I was. For some reason, I didn't think he would believe me.

"Who are you?" he asked.

I stood and offered my hand. "Heila Derby. And you?"

He shook my hand. "Tem Basker." He gestured to the lake. "I study frogs here."

"Do you have warts?"

The question seemed to disturb him. Oh, he was missing Paige. Good boy. "I don't have any." He nodded to where I had been sitting. His gaze lingered on the spot. "What are you doing?" he asked.

"Just resting. I've had a busy week at work."

"Where do you work?"

"At Trio Lab. They're a big genetics firm." I added, "They're connected to the Federation."

"I know the outfit. What do you do there?"

"Oh, I clean test tubes, make little alien monsters. That sort of thing. Do you like studying frogs?"

He glanced back at the lake. He winced as he did so; it seemed as if the whole place were haunted to him. Or maybe it was me who was haunting him.

"To tell you the truth, no, I don't like it anymore," he said.

"Well, then you should quit and work with me," I said.

That amused him. He smiled. "I don't know anything about genetics."

It only struck me then that I was really talking to him. Maybe it was the smile. I felt it better to maintain light banter with him, at least at first. But the sudden realization of the consequences of the meeting almost flattened me. This was Tem! I had struggled through an entire Creation to stand beside him again. It was all I could do not to break down and cry and hug him. I just had to touch him, I thought, even a little. I brushed a water drop from his face. The brief contact sent a thrill through my entire being.

"I could teach you," I said in a shaky voice.

He grabbed my hand as I started to take it back. He had noticed my voice faltering and knew something was going on.

"Have I seen you before?" he asked. "You look so familiar."

I shook my head. "I don't think so, Tem."

43

We went to lunch. I'm not sure who invited whom. Clearly he found me both disturbing and attractive. He kept staring at me. Over our food, he told me more about his work, and asked me for details about mine. I don't know why, but I got rolling on a subject I probably shouldn't have.

"I'm fascinated with cloning," I said. "Human cloning. I think it's our best chance at immortality, at least in the near future. I want to try to find a way to awaken cellular memories. I'm convinced they exist. As part of my research, I'm doing an experiment with dog clones, to see if they can be made to recall the tricks their originals were taught." I paused. "That way, when we're about to die, we can keep cloning ourselves. We can go on practically forever, with all our original memories intact."

He was curious. "If your research ever worked, would you have yourself cloned?"

"Yes. Without hesitation. How about you?"

He shook his head. "I can't imagine two of me."
He paused. "But I can imagine two of you."

"Why's that?"

"I figured out who you remind me of. This girl I know—Paige Christian. You look a lot like her. You even act like her."

"She must be an extraordinary person." I spoke carefully. "Is she a girlfriend?"

He shrugged. I didn't know if I liked being referred to with a shrug.

"I met her six months ago, just before she went off on a deep-space mission with her father." He sighed. "She's aboard the *Traveler.*"

I put a hand to my mouth as if shocked. "Oh no. Were you two close?"

He had a faraway look in his eyes. I liked that.

"Yeah. We spent only a week together, but we got real close." He shook his head. "It was probably a mistake."

"Why do you say that?"

"Isn't it obvious? Because I'm never going to see her again."

"I know that might be painful for you, but the memory of being with her might be worth that pain." I paused. "It's possible."

He shook his head. "You don't understand. You say goodbye to someone in that situation and that's it. By the time she comes back, only a year will have gone by for her, but I'll be dead." He stared down at his coffee. "No. I think it would've been better if we'd never met."

"But you're still able to communicate with each other, aren't you?"

"Yes. When the *Traveler*'s engines turn off, she can receive transmissions. But that only happens once a month for a very brief time." He paused. "But soon she'll be out of reach because their time dilation is about to go wild."

He was different from the Tem I had left, more serious. I kind of liked the change in him. His pain had matured him. No one knew better than I how that worked.

I reached over and took his hand. "Can I be your friend?"

He acted startled. "Sure. But I don't know if I'm the best company right now. As you can see, I have a lot on my mind."

"I don't mind. I'm not here to take Paige Christian's place. I just want to be your friend."

44

My desires were in conflict. It was important to me that Tem maintained his devotion to Paige, and at the same time I wanted more than a platonic relationship. We frequently had lunch, and even began to spend a few evenings together: dinner, a movie, the theater—how I loved to see plays again! It became more and more difficult to keep my distance. Mostly, though, I just wanted to kiss him or hold his hand.

I had waited so long.

Then, perhaps our tenth time going out, it happened. We were down at the beach, walking along the water. The sun had just set—that time of day had a special significance for me, for obvious reasons. I just stopped him and kissed him, and he kissed me back. It was absolute heaven until he turned away wearing a pained expression.

"What's the matter?" I asked. Stupid question.

"I can't," he muttered. "I like you, but I can't."

I touched his arm. "Is it because of her?"

His answer had better be yes.

"Yeah." He gestured helplessly. "When I'm with you, I can't stop thinking about her."

"Maybe that's good," I said quietly.

"No. I can't handle the guilt. I mean, I know she's gone. I know I'm never going to see her again, but I still feel connected to her." He paused and stared out over the sea. "We made a promise to each other."

"What kind of promise?"

He struggled for the words. "We promised to write each other—but that's not what I'm talking about. We made it clear that we would always be there for each other. Even over the many miles and the many years." He lowered his head and I was afraid he might cry, even though I had never seen Tem cry before. "I can't explain how much I love her. It's like our souls are bonded together."

I stroked his arm. "And you feel some of that same bonding when you're with me?"

He nodded reluctantly. "I feel a great deal when I'm with you."

I touched his neck. "You can love me, Tem. You can love me and still love her. I promise you, I know that's true."

He was unconvinced. "I can't sit and write to her if I'm thinking of you." He shook me off and turned away. "It's not right."

"I'm sure your letters mean a lot to her," I said to his back.

He paused and raised his head again, this time to the stars, which were just beginning to come out. He pointed out the plane of the zodiac.

"Do you know much about the cometary cloud?" he asked.

"Yes. It lies just outside the solar system. It's the source of our comets. It's supposed to contain millions of them."

He nodded. "The *Traveler's* out there somewhere. Like I told you, it's only now finally closing in on the speed of light. Do you know how fast that is?"

"One hundred and eighty-six thousand miles a second."

"Yeah," he said sadly. "That's pretty fast. Sometimes I think all the thoughts I have about her can't reach her. That thoughts move at a finite speed, and they can never quite catch up." He chuckled without mirth. "It's a stupid idea, isn't it?"

"No." I stepped to his side, touched his face this time, forced him to look at me. It was time. "You say you made promises to her. Didn't she make promises to you?"

He hesitated. "Yeah."

"You told me you went to Hawaii together. Did she make a promise to you there?"

"Heila, I don't understand why—"

"Did she?" I persisted. "While you lay on the

beach together. Didn't she say something to you while she thought you were asleep?"

There was wonder in his eyes. Maybe I saw the stars there. Maybe he saw the light in my eyes. He suddenly became still.

"Yes," he whispered.

I nodded and quoted myself. " 'I'm going to see you again, after this week. I don't know how, but I will, Tem. I swear it. You're not getting away from me.' " I paused. "She was a strong girl. Neither of you knew how strong." I leaned over and kissed his cheek, whispered in his ear. "It's me, Tem. It is Paige. I came back for you."

He jumped. He grabbed me and held me at arm's length. "It can't be you. It's not possible."

I reached up and touched the tip of my nose, my cheeks. "I had a little plastic surgery so you wouldn't recognize me right away." I chuckled softly. "Please don't ask me how I got here. You wouldn't believe me if I told you."

He was still struggling with the impossible. "But you're older. Even if you were somehow able to get off the *Traveler*—nothing can dilate time backward."

I held a finger to his lips. "Shh. You want more proof, I know. But proof is a quality demanded by the intellect. The heart does not require it. The heart knows, it feels the truth." I paused. "What do you feel?"

What I said had a magical effect on him. Now he wept. "It is you, Paige."

"Yeah. It's me." Drawing him close, kissing him again, I spoke once more in his ear. "You know, in the future, in another life, you're going to be a real smart guy.

45

From then on we were always together, except when we were working or in class. I stood over his shoulder as he wrote letters number seven and eight. I was his guardian angel who knew exactly what Paige was going through as she read the letters. I gave her what warning was permitted. Tem didn't understand why I wanted the letters worded exactly so but that did not matter to me.

My genetics Ph.D. came quickly, before two years were up. But what I handed in as my doctoral thesis was a fraction of what I knew about human DNA. Late at night, in Trio Lab's most sophisticated facility, I conducted experiments that mankind had outlawed a century before. Direct manipulation of the human genetic code to produce a superior breed was forbidden. Mankind had had bad experiences in the past. The genetically superior always wanted to take over.

I thought that should be the least of mankind's worries.

The Shamere. I often dreamed of them.

Three years after returning home I discovered I was pregnant. I wasn't surprised since I had artificially inseminated myself. Not just with sperm, but with cells from Tem's reproductive area that I had taken one night with a long syringe while he lay in drugged sleep.

The baby wasn't Tem's. It *was* Tem.

A clone. It grew in my womb.

I never told him. I couldn't explain how I had passed through the void between Creations to reach him. It was too huge a concept—it wasn't something the human mind could accept, unless one had been in that endless darkness, that absolute silence. Privately, I think he believed we had met a superior race in the future that knew the secret of time travel. I just giggled when he teased me with the idea. For his sake, I realized, the less he knew the better. There were painful days still ahead, hard decisions that had to be made.

Yet I was the same person who had almost murdered the young Paige Christian outside the library. I accepted my destiny while rebelling against it at the same time. But I began to see that my thoughts on the matter were meaningless. Alosha's words had told me as much.

"Along the path there is free will. Once the goal is reached the understanding dawns that everything was destined. But a man or a woman cannot pretend to be at the goal while still on the path. For you, at this time, you must act as if you have free will."

But in reality it did not exist.

Because I had thought I could kill the young Paige, and break the cycle. But the woman who had met me outside the library before *I* left earth had reached in her coat pocket as well. She had frightened me, and with good reason. She had thought to shoot me in the head, but was unable, just as I had been unable.

The cycle was seemingly endless.

I enjoyed being pregnant. The potential mother role reminded of the time right after the Creation began when I felt I was the mother of all things. I had a right, I thought, to enjoy what I could while there was time. When our son was born, I insisted he have his father's name. Tem protested—we would always be confusing them, he said. But that wasn't going to be a problem for me. I loved my son as much as I loved his father. Tem was a wonderful dad.

A year later I gave birth to a daughter.

Tem was elated. She looked just like me.

She was me, my clone. Her nickname was Alpha.

Alpha was a year old when I heard about the *Pandora.*

I applied for a position on the ship. I was the Federation's best genetic scientist. I had helped solve the secret of artificial hibernation. I was accepted immediately, then I made a strong case for why Tem and our children had to come with me. The authorities said yes to my request. They did not enjoy destroying families.

The *Pandora* was supposed to follow the *Traveler*'s path, except it was to be gone as long as five centuries. It was the first sleeper ship—the crew would only be conscious while the actual time dilation was taking place. That was perfect for me, for my plans.

I was a light sleeper.

46

I sat aboard the *Pandora* by Tem's hibernaculum as he slowly began to fall asleep. We were not in the weightless cavern where the hibernaculums would eventually be stored. Each person was put under in a special medical facility located near the bridge. As I watched, Tem's blood circulated via tubing through a computer-controlled purifier. The blood chemistry had to be significantly altered before full hibernation could be induced. I was an expert on the subject. I had designed the purifier myself. Tem's eyes were drowsy as I held his hand and smiled for him.

He didn't know he was never going to wake up.

That his greatest love was going to kill him in his sleep.

It was a forced smile I wore. Yes, my God.

"How are the kids?" he asked as he yawned for the hundredth time.

"You asked that five minutes ago, sleepyhead," I said. "They're fine. They're already both asleep. I oversaw their procedures myself."

"That's good." He squeezed my hand lightly. "Who would have thought when we met beside that lake that we would end up here together? Headed on an adventure mankind couldn't have dreamed of two centuries ago."

I brushed his long dark hair aside. It kept falling in his eyes. "You underestimate those people. Remember I studied that period. They had plenty of dreamers."

He yawned again. "What I mean is that we've come a long way together. Our love has taken us this far, and now we have children to share our love with."

My eyes were damp. "They do belong to us. Nothing's going to take them away from us."

He noted my sorrow. "What's the matter?"

"Nothing. Everything's fine, really."

There was a gleam in his eyes as he stared at me. "You're so beautiful. Did I ever tell you that?"

"Once or twice." I leaned over and kissed his forehead. "Did I ever tell you how you make my universe go round? That without you I'd be nothing? Just dust floating among the stars." I coughed weakly as a tear did roll over my cheek. "Starlight twinkling in the dark."

Tem was concerned. "You're crying. Are you happy or sad?"

I swallowed. "I'm very happy. To have this chance to say good night to you." Reaching over, I kissed him again, on the hand this time. "Good night my love. Sweet dreams. Never forget me."

He smiled. I knew he would wear that smile for billions of years.

"Never is a long time," he said.

Even for us.

I left him then, before he could see me break down.

47

I was not the last one to go to sleep. That was for our senior medical officer. But I would be the first one to wake up. I had personally measured the chemicals that were to be put into my bloodstream and carefully programmed the computer attached to my hibernaculum. I had set an alarm.

For all of mankind. Yet the alarm would ring too late for them.

It was supposed to be a good thing.

I thought of Tem as I fell asleep. The tears froze on my face as the temperature went down. I felt them, even as I lost consciousness, and knew how painful they would be to wipe off when I woke again, just outside the orbit of Pluto.

48

When I did awake I got to work immediately, all alone, in the *Pandora*'s elaborate laboratory. I had brought extensive supplies from earth. Actually, I had little left to do. Everything had been ready for the last year. I merely had to wake the sleeping monsters.

The designers of the *Pandora* had done me a great service. The ship was constructed so that the hibernaculum-containing chamber could be separated from the propulsion end of the vessel. This was a safety feature. For example, if for some reason the engine core became unstable, the sleeping occupants in their chamber could be jettisoned and later picked up by another ship. I planned to separate the parts a little sooner than anyone had expected. The propulsion end would take off for another star—carrying a deadly cargo—and create the nightmare race of all time.

The Shamere. I was their mother as well.

But before I could do that I had to attend to my children. I had to get them off the *Pandora*. More importantly, I had to awaken their memories, let them know exactly who—or *what*—they were. Here was perhaps the biggest hole in my plan, or perhaps its greatest strength. I was assuming I could accomplish such a stirring of memory because I knew the awakening was required by the future I had already experienced. My faith in destiny was extraordinary by this time. I could not let the wolf loose on the universe without also sending out the means to destroy the wolf, which was *me*, my knowledge of Shamere physics. In other words, I was trusting Alosha would return one last time and perform a miracle.

I woke up Alpha and little Tem.

He was four and a half. She was only three.

They stared at me with sleepy eyes.

"Are we there yet?" Tem asked.

"No. Mommy has changed her mind. You're going to earth before Daddy and me. I'm going to send you in a shuttle. You don't have to worry, you won't have to fly it. I have already told the computer on board exactly where to take you. In one week you will be close to the inner planets and someone will come pick you up. I have set the shuttle to send out a distress signal."

My children looked at each other.

"But we want you to come with us," Alpha said.

"Yeah," Tem agreed. "We'll get hungry."

I laughed softly. "You will not get hungry. There

is plenty of food aboard the shuttle. You just have to open it up to eat. But you won't be lonely. Before you leave, Mommy's going to perform a fun experiment with you. After this experiment, you will know a lot more than you do now. You will be as smart as your Mommy and Daddy."

"Will we be big like you?" Alpha asked.

"You will be big where it counts." I paused. "Now sit up straight and close your eyes. Take a few deep breaths through your nose. That's it—relax and keep your eyes closed. Now your Mommy's going to hold your hands. First I'll hold Alpha's, then I'll hold yours, Tem. While I do that, I want you to be happy and know that your Mommy and Daddy love you very much." I took Alpha's tiny hands in mine. "Just keep breathing and don't be afraid."

The miracle started at once.

"Go back . . . In time and space. A ship floats in the void . . . It is another ship . . . The task is not easy but you are equal to it. You have gone through a great deal to arrive at this time and place. You have accumulated tremendous knowledge. You understand the Shamere as no one else can understand them. Their wealth of technology—it belongs to you . . . They are really not so different from you when you remember all that you have learned. The stars help you remember. That is why you love them so much. . . . You remember, Paige Christian?"

I remembered Alosha's words clearly and wondered if I was saying them out loud. Someone was speaking for sure. I was already far away, in a trance state where all I saw were the stars. Yet in this vast space I sensed a great being. For a moment I wondered if it was my daughter, but then I sensed it was closer to me than even she. This being—it was a part of the stars. It lived in them, gave life to them, and in the same way gave life to me. Briefly I wondered if it was who *I* would be in the future, what I would evolve into, if I had the courage to live my life.

Yet the thought struck me as ironic.

My life was all but over.

Yet this being didn't seem to agree with me.

I felt a sharp pang of longing. The presence had moved closer to me, close enough to touch. Now that it was here I couldn't bear to be separated from it. The peace that radiated from it was of cosmic proportions. A torrent of blissful light engulfed me. Suddenly I was not an individual, but an ocean. I washed against a million shores, all in the same instant, and yet I felt absolutely centered. This was a taste of Alosha's state, I knew, and I was grateful for it. Unfortunately, my glimpse of eternity was short lived, perhaps as short as the life of a mortal seemed to a star.

I felt someone shake my hands.

I opened my eyes. Alpha stared at me.

No. I stared at myself. For a moment it was as if I were gazing into a mirror. A shiny reflective surface that split consciousness as well as light. I could see through Alpha's eyes and my own at the same time.

Then she spoke and the mirror shattered into a million pieces. I hardly recognized the voice. . . .

Because it was my own voice.

"It worked," she said calmly. "I know all you know."

I nodded calmly, although I shook inside. "You have my memories until the time I withdrew your seed cells from my body."

Alpha shook her head. "I remember everything you have experienced until now. I am the same as you. There is no difference."

"That's not possible."

"It is a fact."

"But the memory is contained in the cells, in the DNA. That is what we have just awakened."

The reply, as it came out of the tiny mouth, was hard to absorb.

"There must be another mechanism at work. Even now I experience what you experience. I see through your eyes. There is no difference between us." She paused. "You often asked yourself this question: was the soul of the Paige Christian you met on the steps of the library the same as your own soul?"

I nodded. "I wondered if the soul changed from Creation to Creation. If we had to repeat the process of becoming one with the Creation again and again. It never made sense to me that could be true."

"Right now, I believe I share the same soul as you," she said.

"That's a scary thought. What happened to the Alpha of a few minutes ago?"

"I think it was always this way. I think I was just unaware of it."

I reached to take Tem's hands. Incredibly, he was still sitting with his eyes closed, taking deep breaths. It was as if he hadn't heard a word Alpha and I had said. Briefly I wondered if the discussion was actually taking place on the telepathic level, and I was simply too close to Alpha to notice. It was an interesting idea.

Alpha stopped me. I withdrew my hands.

"It won't work for him," she said.

I paused. "How do you know?"

"I know. He will never understand he was Tem. To him, I will always be his sister."

I frowned. "That's not the way I planned it. You were supposed to go on with him by your side. You can't go through what I did."

"I am the same as you. I can go through what you went through."

"But I don't want that. It was horrible."

"It is the way it is."

I paused. "Can you see the future?"

"No. I can only see what you see. But already a difference in perspective has arisen between us. This is because you are about to kill your body, while mine is just beginning to live."

"I am more fragile than you?" I asked.

"Yes." She leaned over and hugged me. What it felt like to hold her right then, I cannot describe. It

was like embracing my soul, but with the awareness
that my soul was going to have to go through hell
again before it would see heaven. A tear fell from
my eye, directly into hers as she stared up at me. It
was as if she absorbed all my sorrows with her
compassionate gaze. "Thank you for my life," she
said.

"Thank you for taking the burden of my life from
me," I replied.

49

The Shamere were a product of human experimen-
tation in genetics. I had realized the truth a long
time before returning to earth. Numerous clues had
helped me solve the mystery. The Shamere knew
our ships, all aspects of our technology. They had
similar DNA. They hated us, for seemingly no
reason. And most of all when I stared into their
eyes I was staring into a slice of my own mind. I
remembered well how the Shamere commander

had hypnotized me on the bridge. I had swooned under her gaze because I had recognized it.

I had seen through the alien's eyes.

Because the alien was me.

After my children were safely away in the shuttle, I accelerated the *Pandora* using a green crystal. Almost immediately a measure of time dilation was achieved, yet I could not push too far into the future because I had to give the Shamere time to grow as a race. To grow so strong that they could smash humanity.

I was the mother of the evil monsters. I had created them in my laboratory on earth by boosting the genetic factors that determined intellect while all but obliterating the DNA codes that gave humanity compassion and understanding. I designed a race of beings for one purpose; to take over the galaxy. Ironically, I used *their* knowledge of genetics to create them, the knowledge I had gained when I had mind linked with the Shamere clone.

Now one might ask which had come first: the chicken or the egg? Me or the Shamere? My answer was that there really was no time, no first or last. I agreed with Alosha. Time was only there to allow us to enjoy the play of Creation. At least until the curtain came down. It had no real substance.

I had used my cells and Tem's to make the alien eggs. The evil commander had obviously been a product of my genetic chain. She had perfect discrimination. She knew what she was there for—to wipe us out. But the friendly alien had been from Tem's cells. I encoded one other thing into my lover's genetic code, before twisting the DNA into the enemy. When the time came, *some* of the Shamere were to help the human beings aboard a ship called *Traveler*. Yes, it was possible to plant a direct message into the genes. The Shamere had shown me how, *after* I had shown them. Perhaps, even, the friendly alien had remembered Tem, before he had died. I liked to think so. I liked to think the alien had sacrificed his life to save someone he loved.

My alien seeds would grow as the propulsion half of the *Pandora* traveled through deep space. The aliens would be born in space. They would grow to adulthood in the emptiness between the stars. That emptiness would color their personalities. But they could *not* choose for themselves where they wanted to build their short-lived dynasty. I had also coded into their genes where they had to settle. They would think they made the choice, but there would be no choice involved. This was necessary so that Alpha would know where to go to destroy them.

And destroy them she would.

She was mankind's life insurance.

But why was I doing all this? Why re-create the nightmare over again? I could say because it was meant to be. Everything was, in a sense. But a more fitting response would be Alosha's.

"The first step toward the truth of the Creation is

discrimination . . . Yet, when you left earth, as a people, perhaps one in a million had achieved discrimination. That is why the destruction of earth occurred. It had to occur, for your own sakes."

I created the Shamere to help mankind grow. Perhaps Judas felt as I did as I stored the seeds aboard the other half of the *Pandora* in special artificial wombs. Yes, the wombs were artificial, but they were still too close to my natural womb for comfort.

I separated the *Pandora*. I watched as the huge starship raced away. The graviton engines left a brilliant streak across the black sky as they displaced a massive gravity wave fueled by green crystals. The sheer demonstration of power was fascinating to behold, but it made me think that if the truth was ever revealed, I would be remembered as the worst murderer of all. I could imagine that Hitler and other tyrants made the same case as I did. Yet I made it anyway.

I was only doing what I had to do.

But I was no Judas, no Hitler.

I did what I did out of love.

There was only love in my heart as I reprogrammed the computer that controlled Tem's hibernaculum. I wept as I worked but I didn't stop. He had to die because I refused to store him like a lump of ice until the end of Creation. I refused to let him wake as a mere mortal, nine billion years from now, when there would be no more time left for him to find eternity. I knew what my change in program would do to my future self. I had been there and known both the blazing hope and the crushing despair.

But I wiped away my tears and killed him anyway.

So that his soul could be set free.

So that when he did meet Paige Christian beside the sea of red dust, he could smile and talk about eternity rather than death. I did all this because of love.

I ruined my own hibernaculum as well, just before climbing inside. I was no faint-hearted hypocrite when it came to destroying life. But as the cold drowsiness swept over me, I wondered if my soul was ever going to be free. I remembered what Alpha had said upon awakening. Her words sent a chill through me deeper than any caused by the hibernaculum.

"Right now, I believe I share the same soul as you."

What did she see now? Through whose eyes?

It made me wonder if I was ever going to die.

It was a curious thought to carry to the grave.

Epilogue

THE LONG TWILIGHT

I was twenty-five years old when we encountered the Shamere warship off Delta-Pau, a blue-red binary star system in the Hercules cluster. I was the same age my mother had been when she left earth in the *Pandora*. Of course, I remember that day, and what followed: how it felt to die in a cold hibernaculum. I even recalled her final musings because she was right—she was not yet free. I was not Alpha, but Paige. The same soul burned in me, the same fire. The war was not over yet.

I left earth with my brother, Tem, fifteen years after the departure of the *Pandora*, as an eighteen-year-old, the same age my mother had been when she left earth in the *Traveler*. We were minor officers aboard a starship called the *Virgo*. Our destination was the star system Ortega-6, in the Felix Nebula. With time dilation, it took us two years to arrive at our goal. But back on earth over three hundred years had elapsed, and therefore the earth was over a century dead. It was the first thing I was told upon waking in my hibernaculum, but naturally I knew of the disaster.

My memory was clear. I knew precisely where the Shamere home planet was to be found. What was left of humanity was grouping together to fight off the Shamere. But it appeared, when I awoke at Ortega-6, that we didn't stand much chance against the enemy.

Throughout my adolescence, on earth, I had kept my remarkable knowledge of science a secret. I reasoned that we had only two weapons against the Shamere: my knowledge of their technology and their ignorance of the fact. I only wanted to reveal what I could when I was in a position to strike a devastating blow. As a result, during my stay at Ortega-6—from the ages of eighteen till twenty-one—I watched many human ships being blown up for want of energy beams and shields I could have built for them. It was a hard test of my discrimination. I had to keep focused on the bigger picture, as my mother had.

But I must stop calling her that.

I am Paige, only Paige tells this story.

At the age of twenty-one I finally did reveal a few secrets I had learned from my long-ago mind link with the Shamere clone. But I didn't tell my superiors everything, only enough to bribe my way—four years later—into the captain's chair of a small cruise ship called the *Jubilee*. People, male or female, young or old, were promoted quickly in those times if they were competent, and I was much more than that. I made my brother, Tem, my Number One, and the first thing we did was fly straight into the arms of the enemy. My superiors didn't want to give me the command for fear of this exact thing. They had wanted to keep their budding physicist superstar out of harm's way. But I had been persistent.

The *Jubilee* was hardly armed for war. It had flimsy shields and only one disrupter cannon. In fact, when we encountered the Shamere warship, we didn't have a single anti-matter torpedo aboard. From the outside we appeared to be helpless, which is the way I wanted to appear. I was not unduly worried that we would be blown out of the sky. As our war had progressed, and the Shamere's victory had become more certain, they had taken to capturing as many prisoners as possible. God knows what they did with them, maybe conducted genetic experiments to de-evolve humanity.

The Shamere warship—as usual—seemed to come out of nowhere. I knew they were able to do this because of their ability to navigate hyperspace, a trick humanity had yet to learn. I had Tem raise shields and arm our disrupter cannon, but I knew we were going to have to surrender.

All the eyes on the bridge were on me, and the eyes were not friendly. I knew what they were thinking. This foolish young captain has led us into this mess. Now we're going to have to kill or be tortured to death. Better to die quickly, and get it over with. . . .

I remembered my father right then, how he was always able to calm his crew in times of emergency. After standing up from my command chair, I strode to the large forward viewing screen. Approaching at high speed, the Shamere warship looked very much like the ones that had smashed the earth: black thorns, tipped with blood. It was odd but I remembered right then how I had scratched my thumb with a thorn in my last incarnation, not long before the Shamere had first appeared. Even now my right thumb still flared up, as if infected.

"We have them now," I said firmly, surprising everyone on the bridge.

"Captain," Tem said, still getting used to using the title for his little sister. "They have us in their sights. They're demanding our immediate surrender."

"That's fine, tell them we surrender," I said. But then I addressed the rest of the bridge. "But don't worry. We are not as helpless as we appear. This ship is equipped with weapons none of you know about. But we will only use them when they think we are down on our knees."

They still looked worried. Tem spoke for all of them. "Where are these weapons, Paige?" he asked.

"Captain," I corrected.

"Captain," he said. "I know nothing of these secret weapons. Where are they stored?"

I patted my pants. "In my pocket. They are small weapons, but nevertheless powerful." I nodded to the approaching warship. "I just have to get aboard that ship. Then I will be able to short out their brain power."

Tem was incredulous. "How?"

"Very simply." I returned to my chair and sat down. "Hail their captain. Tell him or her I wish to come over in a shuttle and discuss the terms of surrender."

"The Shamere never grant terms," Tem said stiffly, obviously dissatisfied with my explanation.

"Then make up something," I replied. "Just get me over to their ship alive."

"They will be coming to drag us all over in a few minutes," Tem muttered. But he turned back to the communication console and began to negotiate what I requested. My brother gave me a hard time, but deep down inside he trusted me. Perhaps his cells did remember a thing or two.

Tem and I were eventually allowed to shuttle over to meet with the Shamere captain. But we never got to the big man. The instant we stepped out of the shuttle airlock and into the warship, I activated the Mazon Beacon in my pocket. I had invented the device. It radiated an intense field of Mazon particles that specifically resonated with the Shamere DNA. Tuned as it was to a particular genetic code, it had no effect on humans. But the armed Shamere guards, who had met us, collapsed writhing on the floor.

They were the enemy, but I hated to see them suffer.

I turned up the intensity so they could die.

Everyone aboard the ship, with the exception of Tem and myself, died.

My brother stared at me as if I were a wicked witch.

"What do you have in your pocket?" he demanded.

I shook my head. "You should ask what I have up my sleeve. Come, we must take command of this vessel."

Tem nodded. "Wait until we get it back to Control."

I stopped him. "We're not taking it to Control. Call for a small crew. We're going to Hydra-9, in the Orion constellation."

"That's a hundred light years from here."

"This ship is fast. It will be there inside the week."

"But what's there?" Tem demanded.

"The Shamere home world."

The statement stunned him. He gazed at me with

haunted eyes. He knew something of my relationship with our mother, although he couldn't possibly guess the real story. But he did believe she spoke to me, sometimes in dreams—as I had told him—and that these dreams were amazingly accurate.

"Did Mother tell you this?" he whispered.

"Yes. The day she died."

"But you were only three." He paused. "How could she have known?"

"Mother was a remarkable woman" was all I said.

Entering Shamere space was easy in one of their ships. The enemy thought we were weak. Not in their wildest imaginations did they believe we could conquer one of their ships. Also, they relied heavily upon the fact that the location of their home world was a secret. For these reasons, they didn't have an elaborate system of security. We were able to pull into orbit around their home world by sending off only a cursory clearance message, which I had pulled out of their computers.

It was then things started to get complicated.

I needed to blow up Hydra-9, the consolidated Shamere power base. Not only did it appear that the majority of the enemy lived on the planet, they had anchored the bulk of their armada in orbit around the world. If Hydra-9 died, the backbone of the Shamere Empire would be crushed.

And I would have fulfilled my purpose in being alive. Again.

I had a box full of green crystals, ripe ones. But to rupture the crust of Hydra-9—as I planned—I had to plant my bomb on the surface of the planet. From orbit the same explosion would do massive damage to the fleet and the planet, but it would not destroy either completely. I wasn't interested in half measures. A chance like we had been given would be rare, even for me. I explained this to Tem as we talked in my quarters, which I had confiscated from the previous captain.

"You may be able to get down to the surface," he said. "But you'll have trouble getting back up to the ship."

"While we are here," I said, "the bomb must go off. That is an unalterable fact."

He regarded me suspiciously. "You see this as a suicide mission. You don't plan on coming back."

"I would like to return alive. But the safest way to see that the bomb explodes where I want it is to detonate it myself."

He was disturbed. "How can you say the *safest* way?"

I reached over and took his hand. This was harder for him, I realized, because he was younger than I. Really, I was twice his age, and I knew better what was at stake.

"It is safest for humanity," I said. "How can I think of myself at a time like this?" I paused. "I can't even think of you, and that is hard."

"You will be recognized the instant you land," he said.

"No. I have made a genetically designed costume. I will get by long enough to plant the bomb."

"But you don't have to stay to detonate it. You can set a timer on it."

"They might remove the timer," I said.

"You can rig it so that if they do, the bomb automatically goes off."

"They are shrewd, these monsters. Who knows how they might be able to disarm the bomb? No, I can't risk it. After I land, after I set the bomb, I detonate it."

Tem was grim. "If you want to be so certain, why don't you just ram the planet now with this ship? The bomb you have constructed would detonate just the same. The crust would rupture. The Shamere would die."

I shook my head. "I will not have your life and the lives of my crew on my conscience. As soon as I land on the planet, you are to take this ship out of orbit." I paused. "That's an order, brother."

Of course Tem didn't listen to me. I should have guessed. I was heading for the surface of Hydra-9 in a Shamere shuttle, ignoring every demand from the alien headquarters for a clearance code, when I became aware of a figure standing behind me. I didn't have to turn to recognize the breathing. Actually, I was too upset to look. One of my major consolations in doing this horrible deed was that my brother would be safe—hopefully for the rest of his life. Now that comfort was gone. I could not very well turn around and head back for the warship. It would just make us that much more suspicious. As it was, I believed we were on the verge of being shot out of the sky.

"Dumb," I said quietly.

He sat beside me. "That I stowed aboard? Or that I have you for a sister?"

I shook my head. "You're going to die for no reason."

He put a hand on my shoulder. "You need me. I can guard you while you set the bomb."

"You'll only call attention to us while I set the bomb. You don't have a Shamere costume."

"Yeah, but they're so ugly. Who wants to wear one of those things anyway?"

I had to smile. For a moment, I heard the Tem of my youth speaking.

My first youth. When he used to kiss me.

"You are dumb for being my brother." I nodded to the space station below us. "We have to come in there."

"Why not just land on a field somewhere?" Tem asked.

"It would make us that more obvious. I believe there are weapons pointed at us this very second. But if we come in smoothly, and don't disobey their directional beacons, I believe they'll let us land."

"Then what?" Tem asked.

"Then there will be a bunch of armed guards waiting for us the instant we step outside this shuttle."

Tem gripped the hand laser he wore on his hip. "Good. My company will come in handy, after all.

"No. I'm going to use my Mazon Beacon again."

"What's the range of that thing?" Tem asked.

"I don't know. Maybe two hundred yards."

"They can shoot you from farther away than that." He paused. "Why should we leave the ship at all? Why not just detonate the bomb the second we land?"

"It will take me a few minutes to bring the bomb up to full power. No, we have to take out the guards who plan to meet us. Then we have to keep the rest of them off our backs until the bomb goes off."

"If anyone has to stay with the bomb, it will be me," Tem said.

"We'll see," I said.

I didn't even bother with the costume. With Tem, my unwelcome partner, it was useless. The moment

we landed we stepped outside and ran into ten
armed Shamere. I activated the beacon and they
dropped dead on the floor. They shrieked as they
died. It was not a pleasant sound.

We were in an incredibly huge structure, perhaps
the main Shamere spaceport. In our immediate
vicinity was a complex network of halls and doors.
The design was honeycombed—it reminded me of
an insect's dwelling. The lighting was a gruesome
red—it was always late twilight on Hydra-9.

The Shamere didn't know how late it really was.

We raced from the shuttle and hid in what
appeared to be a maintenance supply closet. I did
not notice any cameras, but feared the whole area
might be watched. We closed the door and Tem
welded the lock in place with his laser. I knelt on
the floor and set to work on the bomb. It resembled
a huge glass beaker, filled with green crystals and
gray slime. I had teased the crystals toward critical
mass. It was only the thick solution I had soaked
them in that kept them from exploding. Using a
tiny internal pump, I began to siphon off the
solution as Tem watched. His forehead was damp
with sweat but otherwise he appeared calm. He was
a brave man, my brother.

I didn't realize how brave he was.

"How do you detonate the bomb?" he asked.

I pointed to a black button on the side of the
beaker. "I will press that when the crystals begin to
bubble."

"And there's enough power in those things to rupture this planet's crust?"

"Yes. More than enough." I glanced up. "I want you to leave now."

"I'm not leaving without you."

I hardened my tone. "We've discussed this. I cannot leave this bomb until it goes off. I didn't know you were coming. I haven't even rigged it with a timer." I paused. "Get back to the shuttle now. The Shamere focus must be here now. You might be able to escape while they're trying to get to me."

"No way. I'm your guard."

"I don't need a guard! I need a brother to live and tell our story! Get out of here!"

Naturally, I expected him to argue with me some more. What he did next caught me completely by surprise. I guess I wasn't so smart, after all.

Tem took out his laser pistol and shot himself in the foot.

No, he carefully amputated his foot from his leg.

Blood poured over the floor as he toppled.

Horrified, I caught him as he fell. "Tem!" I cried. "Why did you do that?"

Now his forehead was soaked with sweat. Lying on the floor in my arms, he struggled to catch his breath. The sight of all that blood couldn't have been easy for him. It wasn't easy for me—I felt it drenching my pant legs.

"I won't be able to walk back to the shuttle," he said. "You have to leave me."

"I'm not leaving you." I reached for his leg. "We need to make a tourniquet. We need to stop the bleeding."

He stopped me. "There's no time. I will bleed to death anyway." He drew in a ragged breath as the puddle of red fluid continued to grow around us. Intellectually, it was one thing to know how many quarts of blood the human body held. But it was quite another to see them spurt out of the body of a loved one. Already he was losing strength. "I have at most a few minutes," he whispered. "You have to go."

There were tears in my eyes. "But I can't leave you. You're all I have in this cold universe."

"Our crew on the Shamere warship we highjacked—I told them not to leave orbit until you returned." A spasm shook him. It went through his whole body and he trembled in my arms. "You have to go back if you're to save them."

"That's nonsense. I gave them orders to leave."

His voice was strained. "They look up to you, Paige. They love you. They will not leave you. Please believe me."

The trouble was, I did believe him. Never before —in both my lives—did I feel so torn. Beside us on the floor, inside the beaker, the green crystals began to fizzle. Two minutes had elapsed since we had killed the guards. More Shamere must be on their way. The door would explode any second. The sight of Tem's blood—I couldn't bear it. And I had my duty to perform.

I reached for the black button.

Tem stopped me. "No, Alpha," he gasped.

I was frantic. "It's too late. It's over, for all of us."

Somehow he managed to force a smile. "Not for you. You have magic. I remember that time aboard the *Pandora,* when mother left us. You thought I was off in my own world, but I remember . . ." His voice trailed off and his eyes lost their focus.

I forgot the button. I shook him. "What do you remember?"

Suddenly it was the most important thing in the Creation to know what was in his memory. It had not been an easy life, living beside a brother I wanted for my husband. But never, in all these years, had I allowed an incestuous gesture or word to pass between us, for my sake as well as his.

Tem's gaze took on a faraway quality as he struggled back to that time aboard the *Pandora* when my mother and the Creation had touched me. But perhaps I misunderstood the depth of his vision. A sudden clarity entered his voice, a tone I had never heard before, even as the blood continued to drain from his body.

"I remember a beach in a place called Hawaii," he said softly. "It was a tropical island. You were lying beside me in the sand and I was pretending to sleep. And you leaned over and whispered in my ear that you were going to see me again after the week was over. You didn't know how but you swore you would."

I wept. "Yeah. I said, 'You're not getting away from me.'"

He smiled again, faintly. "Yes, That's it." He paused. "Did that really happen? It seems so real."

My tears splashed over his face. "Yes, Tem. I happened. It was real. It was another life. This is not the first time you and I have been together."

His gaze was again distant. "I see something else. A huge red sun, an endless plain choked with dust. The sun is going down and we're sitting on a bluff and everything around us is so still, so quiet. We can't even hear ourselves breathing. And I say to you, 'Time is nothing to us, Paige.' And you agree. You say, 'This moment is forever.'" He stared at me with the innocence of a child, the innocence of Alosha. "Did that really happen?" he asked.

I squeezed his hands. "It will happen, Tem. We'll meet again on that world. That's the earth. I'll see you there and we'll talk about old times."

He was impressed. "The earth is still there? Our home?"

"Yes, Tem. Our home is still there." Leaning over, I kissed him on the forehead. The Creation may have moved me then, but I suddenly knew he was right. I had to leave. I could not let my crew die. I pressed the laser gun in his hands and whispered in his ear. "I will never forget you."

He reached up and touched the side of my face. "Never is a long time."

I pressed his hand to my cheek. There was blood on it.

"Not for us," I said.

The highjacked Shamere warship was still far off when I knew Tem was about to push the black button. It may have been a telepathic message he sent me. The certainty was strong enough. I radioed ahead for my crew to get out of orbit. I would do the same and rendezvous with them soon.

Shamere shuttles were not gravity compensated. Bringing the small craft's twin thrusters up to full power, I accelerated so rapidly I almost blacked out. The stars spun—I didn't even know if I was heading in the right direction.

Behind me there was a tremendous flash of light. I was reminded of my lonely days aboard the *Traveler* during the darkness after the stars died, how the loneliness ended with a similar flash of light, when the next Creation began. But this was not the light of creation but the flames of destruction.

Still, there was great promise in it.

As the crust of Hydra-9 ruptured and the unimaginable energy of the mantle was liberated, the planet was torn apart and the Shamere fleet was crushed. Smoothing out my own wobbly course and watching the death of the Shamere Empire, I thought that the last nightmare of mankind's childhood was finally over. Now the way was clear for the third step on Alosha's seven-rung ladder. The top still looked far away, but I believed as a people we would now reach it.

My days as a warrior and an important person were over. I returned to Ortega-6 and handed the Shamere warship over to my superiors. There were still a few Shamere vessels out in space causing mischief, but their home base was gone and soon they would fall. My superiors immediately set to dismantling the warship and learning all its secrets. They didn't need help from me.

My crew tried to tell what was left of humanity that I was a hero, but it was an honor I managed to avoid by living quietly alone and then leaving Ortega-6 three years later and traveling incognito through the galaxy aboard another exploratory vessel. This one was called the *Pulsar,* and she was fast, with her new hyperdrive, courtesy of Shamere technology. Once again, I went by the name of Alpha Book. It had begun to grow on me.

We visited many planets, and I eventually jumped ship at a planet called Cirgo-2, in the Pleiades cluster. The place fascinated me because there was an indigenous race of homo sapiens already living there. Where they came from no one could imagine, but they looked exactly like us except for their light blue skin. As a race, they were somewhat primitive. The closest comparison I could make to their culture would have been the early American Indians. They dressed and danced like the ancient Hopis.

Yet to me they were far from primitive. There were numerous tribes scattered over Cirgo-2, and although their speech and individual customs varied, they all lived peacefully together. In fact, the planet was very much as North America must have been before the white man arrived. There were lush forests, breathtaking deserts, wide open plains, and rugged mountain ranges.

I ended up staying with a tribe that lived between the mountains and the desert. They were called the Shanti and didn't mind my white skin. They accepted everything. Indeed, the whole concept of space travel didn't impress them. According to their colorful legends, their ancient ancestors used to journey through space all the time. The Shanti had simply given up the burden of the technology when they became truly civilized. They were much happier without it, they said, and I believed them.

For the first time in a long time, I discovered I was happy.

I learned their language effortlessly, and my days

were simple. I awoke when the sun rose and worked in the garden until noon. Then I swam in a nearby river and ate a meal of ground corn and milk and beans and fruit. These foods were similar to those on earth, except the corn was always blue. Often I hiked in the hills by myself, or else helped the village men and women weave one of the many tapestries that they were always producing.

Actually, I found the weaving addictive. I could spend hours working on a new design. I seemed to slip into a trance at such times, not noticing the hours that passed. After a year or so in the Shanti village, I found myself automatically weaving in the images I glimpsed as the Creation had begun. The mass of energy liberated at that time had not been an incoherent blur. I seemed to remember it better now, with eyes and a soul that were no longer oppressed with the burden of a seemingly impossible destiny. How the whirlpools of gas had formed into glorious mandalas as they began to cool into galaxies. How the stars had glimmered like polished jewels as they took birth in the black nebula. All these visions I wove into my tapestries, and as I did so, I would have moments where I could feel the presence of Alosha. Sometimes I thought the cosmic being would speak. But if it did, it did so in silence.

The village people whispered among themselves as I laid my tapestries out on the cool sand to be admired. I was white—I was from another star system. But that didn't impress them. My tapestries did, however. I wasn't sure why.

One day the village chief came to me as I was returning from a long hike in the hills. He was actually only chief in title—he never ordered anyone to do anything. If he had done so, the rest of the tribe probably would have laughed at him. The Shanti didn't have many rules, and only had a chief for special occasions. He would sometimes decide which god they should dance to on a particular holiday. But if the tribe didn't like his suggestion, he was quick to change his mind. He was tall and old and he had a radiant smile, although he was missing a few front teeth. He always seemed especially fond of me.

"Alpha," he said. "I have received an important invitation from our High Elder. He would like to meet you in his cave."

I had not heard the High Elder title before. "Where is his cave?"

The chief nodded to the tall mountains to our east. "Up there. It's a five-day hike from here. I would accompany you there, but it isn't allowed. But I can draw you a map and help you gather supplies for the journey. It's far but the way isn't dangerous."

I laughed. "Wait a second. I don't know if I want to go. Five days of walking up a mountain to meet an old man I don't know. That doesn't sound like fun."

The chief was surprised at my tone. "The High Elder is not old. We call him Elder because he is wiser than the rest of us. But it's important, Alpha, that you see him. He seldom sends an invitation to speak to anyone. It's considered a great honor that he's chosen you."

"But why does he want to see me? Is it because I'm not from here?"

"Oh no. That's unimportant. It's because of your tapestries."

I laughed again. I did so more often those days. "What's so special about my tapestries?" I asked.

The chief's eyes grew wide. "The Elder has seen a couple of them. He says they contain the secrets of life."

I thought for a moment. How could the Elder know that?

"I'll go see this man," I told the chief.

I set off the next morning. Almost immediately, as I hiked into the mountains, a remarkable thing happened. Something totally unexpected and very disturbing.

It was usual for me to be gone an entire day hiking alone in the hills. I preferred to be alone when I hiked. I loved to listen to the wind in the trees, to soak up the smell of the flowers, to feel the dirt beneath my feet.

Yet this time as I walked into the mountains, I felt heavy at heart. I realized quickly it was because

I was sad to be leaving the Shanti. They had been my family for the past year, and even though I knew I would see them again in a few days, I felt as if I was being cut off from my security net. In fact, much to my horror, I began to feel the *exact* emotions I had when I first left the earth, when I said goodbye to Tem. I knew it was ridiculous but I couldn't will the emotions away. Yet it had been years since such feelings plagued me. And I thought I was over such mundane human sentiment. Tears formed in my eyes and I kept glancing over my shoulder, hoping to find perhaps that the chief or one of the women of the village had decided to follow me.

But there was no one there.

The whole first day of my hike, I felt terribly alone.

That night I camped in a rocky hollow, where there was shelter from the wind. Staring up at the stars, I though of all the loved ones I had lost up there. What were they now? Stardust, floating atoms in cosmic currents that circled the galaxy once every million years. No matter how hard I tried to hold on to love, I thought, the Creation had taken it away. Yet I couldn't stop gazing at the stars. They were so beautiful, and I craved the feeling of nostalgia they brought. At least they were real, I thought.

I dreamed of Tem, Kabrina, and my father that night.

The next day I felt lighter. Indeed, I wondered about my emotional attack the previous day as the mountain peaks ahead drew me. There was a new bounce in my step, new energy in my stride. No longer did I look back. I was anxious to find the High Elder, to speak to him about my life. I hoped perhaps he could shed some light on why I had been chosen to live so long, and suffer the death of the same love again and again.

That night I camped near a cave. I built myself a fire to keep warm and make my tea. To my surprise, several small animals gathered at the perimeter of the light cast by the burning logs. They were similar to raccoons, foxes, and squirrels. Once again I was puzzled about how so many of the species of earth appeared in almost the same form on this world. I did not believe the Shanti's tales of past space adventures. From experience, I knew that many primitive tribes boasted of the incredible abilities of their ancient ancestors.

These animals seemed unafraid of my fire. It was only after a while I realized their desire for my food outweighed any reservations they had about the crackling logs. Holding out pieces of bread, I coaxed the animals to my side. Soon I had a whole group of critters sharing my evening meal. They felt like family to me. I loved each of them, and made sure that each was given something to eat. Their warm fuzzy faces, as they stared at me, filled me with love.

My third day of hiking was meditative. I didn't look around. I kept walking, kept my focus on my breathing. Several times during the day, I felt the presence of Alosha. That night I built another fire, in a meadow in a thick part of the forest, and worked on a small tapestry. It was to be of Tem, and I struggled with it at first, unable to decide how to portray him. But then a voice seemed to speak from inside me. Relax, Paige, weave what comes. There is no need to think too much about it. There is really no need to think at all.

I worked half the night, lost between waking and dreaming. All the time I felt both charged with inspiration and deeply relaxed. In the morning I was stunned to see how rich the tapestry was. It was one of my finest—the colors and composition combined to form magic. Tem was sitting on a rock on the other side of a tidal pool, staring down into the blue water, which splashed with life. It was a classic scene, yet the expression on his face intrigued me. I don't know if I could have consciously decided on it. It was a cross between that of the mischievous young man I had met in the park and the omniscient god I had found on dying earth.

But his eyes were left incomplete. I had faltered when it came to them. They would be the hardest part, if I was ever to finish it.

But I thought, if I completed the tapestry in time, I could give it to the High Elder. Several times, while hiking, I had regretted not bringing a gift for him.

The fourth day I began to have trouble with the chief's map. Before leaving I questioned him about it, but he kept reassuring me that there was no chance of my getting lost. Now it looked more than likely. The map said I was to turn left when I came to the Three-Headed Hills and then right when I reached the Wolf Tree. Well, I did find some hills that had three peaks, but they didn't resemble three heads. Then I came to a tree that was kind of scary looking, but I only turned right there because there was no other tree in the vicinity. For the next few miles, I figured my journey had been in vain because I was surely lost in the mountains. Briefly I wondered if I would be able to find my way back to the Shanti village.

But then, out of the blue, I didn't care. I was following the map as well as I possibly could and couldn't allow myself any regrets. I understood my responsibility was to try, as best as possible, to get to the cave. That was it. With this understanding my mind was put totally at ease. I wasn't responsible for whether I succeeded or failed in my mission. If the High Elder was anxious to meet me, and he was so wise, he could find me.

That night, my fourth in the mountains, I slept deeply.

On the fifth day I became preoccupied with the idea of writing a book about my life. The possibility had occurred to me before, of course, but I had always dismissed it because I didn't think anyone would believe what I had to say. As I walked, I began to understand that I hadn't recorded my story because I was afraid of being ridiculed. And here I had always convinced myself I was too humble to seek out the spotlight. Now I understood that to move center stage required courage. That others could learn from my experiences. God knows I had learned from them.

That day I cut my hike short and started on this story with paper and a pen from the *Jubilee*. The whole time with the Shanti, I had kept the stationery tools close to me, perhaps superstitiously, still half believing that I owed Tem another letter. But now as I sat down beside a roaring fire, I began to write him a real love letter. My whole life had been an uninterrupted act of loving him. Tears came as I wrote, but not all were sad. Many were stirred by feelings of gratitude. So often during my chaotic life I had believed myself cursed by God. Now I saw that I had been incredibly lucky. The fact that I was still alive said it all.

On the sixth day I drew close to where the High Elder was supposed to live. The chief's map had turned out to be accurate, after all, and my faith in it had been rewarded. I came to the Seven Waterfalls—as described—and then turned right at the Bald Rock, which did indeed look like a bald man's head. From there I only had to follow a ravine that would dead end at the High Elder's cave. There was no chance of getting lost now.

Another realization swept over me as I hurried forward. They were getting somewhat embarrassing with their frequency. Perhaps the thin mountain air was affecting my brain, although I did feel alert and full of energy.

Finally, I saw that there had never been a chance of getting lost. I just knew this. I couldn't explain how I knew it. Something had been guiding me all along. Perhaps it had been the High Elder.

I knew I was reaching the end of the path.

The walls of the ravine grew high on both sides.

But the big man was not there when I reached the cave.

There was only a boy, maybe ten years old. He was gathering herbs when I arrived. He looked up and smiled at my approach. He had a pleasant expression. His skin was a much deeper blue than the average Shanti. I wondered if he was from another tribe. His hair was long and dark, his big eyes as black as deep space. I held out my hand as I walked up to him. We shook hands—on many planets throughout the galaxy it was the best way to say hello.

"My name is Paige Christian," I said in my best Shanti. "I was told by the chief of the Shanti to come here. I heard the High Elder wants to talk to me." I gestured to the cave. "Is he in there?"

The boy shook his head. "No. He is not there."

"Is he in the area somewhere?"

"Yes."

"Do you know when he will return?"

"Soon."

"Today maybe?"

"Maybe. He never goes far when he leaves." The boy gestured to the cave. "May I make you some tea?"

"Yes, thank you. I'm tired from my long hike."

"Let me take your bag," he said, reaching out. He was not a tall boy but he was well muscled. I let him take my supplies.

"Thank you," I said again. "What is your name?"

"Keshava."

"I like that name. Does it mean something in particular?"

"Long haired."

"Well, that's perfect for you. You have very long hair."

He smiled shyly. "You have red hair."

I brushed my hair out of my eyes. "Yeah, and I have white skin. I bet you haven't seen many like me around here."

We walked toward the cave opening. "There have been a few like you," he remarked.

"Really?" I was astounded. "When?"

"A long time ago," he said.

* * *

Keshava made me tea and we relaxed by the fire at the mouth of the cave. I chatted about my adventures along the road and he listened patiently. He had a particular way of staring at me that made my words flow freely. But after a while it began to get dark, and my disappointment at not seeing the High Elder was stronger than I could have imagined. A sense of loneliness returned. Not wishing to bother the boy, I reached for my bag. I took out my tapestry. I thought if I could finish the thing tonight, I could give it to the High Elder tomorrow, assuming the man showed up. I wanted him to see Tem with his own eyes, through my eyes. Keshava stared at my tapestry without blinking.

"That is very nice," he said.

"Thank you." I spread it on the ground between us. The sun had just set; it was going to be a cold night. We were at a high elevation. Indeed, the air suddenly seemed as thin as it had on earth at the end of time. Not that I experienced any trouble breathing. I smoothed out my work of art. I could have been watching a movie of the two of us sitting beside the fire. I tried to push away the mental image but it was stubborn. I nodded to Tem's face on the tapestry. "I'm having trouble with the eyes," I said.

"Why do you say that?" Keshava asked.

"I'm just dissatisfied with the way they are. They're incomplete somehow. But I'd like to finish it tonight, if I could, and give it to the High Elder."

"Then finish it."

I sighed as I stared at Tem's face. "I don't think I can."

"Why not?"

I smiled to myself. "I think I'm still too close to the subject matter to see it clearly."

"What you wish the most, clouds your vision the most."

I glanced up.

"What you most wish for, what you most hope for—that is your greatest illusion. The greatest barrier that separates you from the Creation."

"Did the High Elder say that?" I asked.

"Yes."

"That's interesting. I heard it before somewhere." I paused. "Your master must be very wise."

The boy continued to stare at me. "You're wise."

I chuckled. "I don't think so." I started to put the tapestry away. "I know nothing."

Keshava stopped me. "No. Finish the work. You're almost done." He added, "It would be a shame not to finish when you're so close."

Something in his voice made me pause. "But I told you, I don't know how to do the eyes."

"What do you want in the eyes?" he asked.

"A certain light." I shrugged. "I saw it once before, but it's hard to remember exactly what it was like." I closed my eyes and put my hand to my head, feeling a pressure there. "It was a long time ago, Keshava."

"Paige," he said softly.

"Yes?" I opened my eyes and glanced at him. He had a special way of speaking—it was almost as if I heard his voice inside my head. "What is it?"

"It wasn't so long ago," he said.

"What wasn't? That I saw this light? Yeah, it was. It would be hard to explain how long ago it actually was."

"No." He leaned forward and touched my hand. His fingers were remarkably warm. The warmth traveled up my arm and into my heart. I felt the chill of the approaching night recede. "You're almost done," he repeated. "You can see the light whenever you choose to see it."

"Oh God," I whispered, finally understanding. I could not tear my gaze from him. I didn't want to. His black eyes abruptly swelled, until I felt as if I was staring into the abyss before the Creation began. This was not a simple boy who sat across from me. He was the High Elder, a being who was one with the Creation. There was unfathomable darkness inside him, but also effulgent light. I could see both extremes in his luminous eyes. And I understood the meaning of his words. He was asking me to place what was inside his eyes into the tapestry, into the fabric of my own life.

He blinked once, probably on purpose, and I

finally caught my breath, and was able to speak again. "You're him," I gasped.

"As are you. There is only one of us." He paused. "You are very near the Creation, Paige Christian."

I shook my head. "No. I'm lost in it. I haven't completed the seven steps that were spoken of before. I don't even know what the last five steps are."

"But you do. You told them to me this evening. You experienced each of them on the walk here."

"No. I don't understand." I reached for his hand. "Will you help me understand, Keshava?"

"I can only tell you what you already know. That is why the Creation did not tell you and your friends all the steps earlier. They would have made no sense to you." He paused. "Now you are wise. You can recite them to me."

I felt humbled. Bowing my head, I spoke in a whisper, knowing he would hear me clearly enough.

"I am unworthy to tell you anything," I said. "Please, you speak."

"As you wish." He paused. "Discrimination is first. Through all your trials, you have learned this well. Even to come here, you had to leave behind that which gave you comfort. But you dropped your attachment to the unreal and you kept walking. You knew there was a greater reality in front of you, that which does not change. The Creation.

"Then there is kindness, giving, service. These are words for the same thing. Kindness is strongest

when discrimination is firmly established. Then
you give without expectation of reward. On the way
here you gave to little animals, and only because
you loved them.

"The third step is spiritual practice. All practice
has one goal—to go inside and come closer to that
which does not change. This is meditation. Your
meditation is weaving your tapestries. As you do
so, you lose all sense of body consciousness. Specif-
ic practices may vary, but they all have this goal.
For a long time now, you have been a master of the
third step.

"The fourth step is faith, an intuitive trust in the
design of the Creation. You had to have that faith to
accomplish what you did in your life. You had to
have faith to follow your map and reach this spot.
The fact that you now sit before me means you
have passed this difficult test.

"The fifth step is to give what you have learned to
those who don't know it. To rise to the top of the
ladder, you must turn and help lift up those below
you. Your story does that. It is the reason you write
it. You have compassion for those who struggle on
the path.

"The sixth step is said to be the most difficult,
but you have already conquered it. It is the illusion
of doership. People think they act, they think they
decide. This keeps them bound. In reality, the
Creation carries out all manner of things. Everything is destined. But this knowledge only comes to
one who nears the end of the path. At the beginning

of the search, it can lead to confusion. So I tell you this in private. It is not something to share with everyone. But you have seen again and again that you do not act."

I nodded. "I could not even shoot myself outside the library, although I tried."

He agreed. "It was not possible." He paused. "It took you six days to climb this mountain. Each day you relived one step on the path. Now the day grows late. Soon, as the world turns and the stars change, another day will begin. You have come to the seventh step. I can give it to you now. It is only now that it will have meaning for you. Before the first six steps are mastered, the seventh step is meaningless. For it is the most simple step of them all, and also the most profound. Listen attentively, it can only be imparted by a man or woman who is one with the Creation." He paused. "Would you like me to give it to you now?"

I bowed again. "Yes. If you feel I'm worthy."

He gestured for me to stare into his eyes. "Look deep, Paige Christian. See yourself in my eyes. See yourself as I see you. The seventh step is a child's expression." He paused again, and a long time seemed to seep into that pause. It was as if it were a crack in the eternal flow of evolution. For a moment I saw the black between the death and birth of the stars, then there was a flash. It came out of the depth of his eyes, from a place I thought I alone had seen.

But he had seen it as well. He spoke softly.

"You are the Creation."

I tried to move my head. To shake it. To say no.

"You are the Creation," he repeated.

No. Not me. I am just a lonely young woman.

But then, staring into his amazing eyes, I didn't feel so lonely.

In fact, I suddenly felt as if I belonged to all things.

"You are the Creation," he said a third time.

Finally, I believed him.

Seven days later I left the mountains and moved into the desert, far from the Shanti village. Moving effortlessly across the wide expanse of the sand, I felt no need to rest or drink. The sun burned before me. The desert was much hotter than the mountains or the Shanti homeland. But as I moved, I smiled and sang to myself and enjoyed the simple pleasures of breathing and being alive.

Time passed, maybe a little, maybe a lot.

The sand beneath changed to blood red. The sun also turned a sober crimson and swelled in size so that it dwarfed the horizon. I could stare at it without pain. This world suddenly seemed so old but there was a satisfaction in the ancient feeling. It was as if a good life were finished and everything that had been planned at the beginning had been accomplished.

Dust stirred before me, tossed by an unexpected gust, and a shape took form in a dark cloud. The matter metamorphosed to life, and there was a person. He nodded and walked toward me. I held out my arm in welcome and when he was close enough he took my hand.

"Alosha," he said.

I had to smile. "Tem."

He put his finger to my lips. "Shh. No one is supposed to know."

Holding hands, we turned and walked into the sunset.

If you have enjoyed this book,
you might also like other books by
CHRISTOPHER PIKE

THE LAST VAMPIRE
stories

Christopher Pike

The Last Vampire

Beautiful and brilliant, Alisa Perne is the last vampire.
For 5,000 years she has hunted alone. Living among
humans, living off humans. Nobody knows her secret.
Or so she thinks.
But someone is stalking her, someone she thought was
long dead. His sole purpose now is to destroy her.
Alisa must make the final, terrible decision between her
own life and the life of the one she loves.

The Last Vampire 2, Black Blood

Alisa and Ray are the last vampires – or so they think.
But now the evil plague is spreading. A brutal murderer is
terrorising Los Angeles. He's hungry for blood – and power.
Has Alisa the power to stop him?
Or will he destroy her first?

The Last Vampire 3, Red Dice

Alisa's secret is out.
She has survived the years – the centuries – undetected.
But now she and her partner Joel are on the run.
The government wants their blood. Their vampire DNA.
But Alisa knows the strength of vampire blood.
The evil it can do. And she will not let it spread –
no matter what the cost.

The
REMEMBER ME
stories

Christopher Pike

Remember Me

Shari didn't understand that she was dead.
Until she followed her family to the morgue and saw
herself lying on a cold slab.
The police said it was suicide. Shari knew she had been
murdered. Shari vows to find her killer – and comes face
to face with a nightmare from beyond the grave.

Remember Me 2: The Return

Jean Rodrigues should be dead.
She fell from a thirty foot balcony and survived.
Her body has healed, but her mind has changed.
Something – or someone – draws her to Shari Cooper's
neighbourhood, a place she's never visited before, but
knows so well. To the spot where Shari died. But Shari
isn't gone forever.

Remember Me 3: The Last Story

Shari is dead. But her soul lives on in Jean Rodrigues,
the talented writer and inspiration to young people
throughout the world. Then one night a mystical story
comes to Shari. A fable that warns her of the destruction of
humanity by creatures who despise mankind. Creatures
who cannot let this story be told.
Creatures who cannot let Shari survive.

THE LOST MIND

Christopher Pike

A girl wakes up in the woods. She has no memory of how
she got there. Or who she is. There is blood on her clothes.
A knife by her hand. Then she sees the body. Why can't
she remember what happened?
Who – or what – has stolen her mind?

FALL INTO DARKNESS

Christopher Pike

Ann Rice is dead. Her best friend, Sharon McKay, is
accused of her murder. The two girls were alone together
when Ann fell off the cliff. But there is no body. And
Sharon's only defence is that Ann committed suicide. But
everyone knew Ann was not the suicidal type. And they're
right. Ann was much more than suicidal.
She was obsessed.

All Hodder Children's books are available at your local bookshop or newsagent, or can be ordered direct from the publisher. Just tick the titles you want and fill in the form below. Prices and availability subject to change without notice.

Hodder Children's Books, Cash Sales Department, Bookpoint, 39 Milton Park, Abingdon, OXON, OX14 4TD, UK. If you have a credit card you may order by telephone – (01235) 831700.

Please enclose a cheque or postal order made payable to Bookpoint Ltd to the value of the cover price and allow the following for postage and packing:

UK & BFPO – £1.00 for the first book, 50p for the second book, and 30p for each additional book ordered up to a maximum charge of £3.00.

OVERSEAS & EIRE – £2.00 for the first book, £1.00 for the second book, and 50p for each additional book.

Name..

Address...

....

....

If you would prefer to pay by credit card, please complete:
Please debit my Visa/Access/Diner's Card/American Express (delete as applicable) card no:

Signature...

Expiry Date...